SUPER NOVA

JAYNE RYLON

eBook ISBN: 978-1-941785-36-2
Print ISBN: 978-1-941785-68-3

Ebook Cover Art By Angela Waters
Photography By Sophia Renee
Print Book Cover Art By Jayne Rylon
Interior Print Book Design By Jayne Rylon

OTHER BOOKS BY JAYNE RYLON

DIVEMASTERS
Going Down
Going Deep
Going Hard

MEN IN BLUE
Night is Darkest
Razor's Edge
Mistress's Master
Spread Your Wings
Wounded Hearts
Bound For You

POWERTOOLS
Kate's Crew
Morgan's Surprise
Kayla's Gift
Devon's Pair
Nailed to the Wall
Hammer it Home

<u>Hotrods</u>

King Cobra
Mustang Sally
Super Nova
Rebel on the Run
Swinger Style
Barracuda's Heart
Touch of Amber
Long Time Coming

<u>Compass Brothers</u>

Northern Exposure
Southern Comfort
Eastern Ambitions
Western Ties

<u>Compass Girls</u>

Winter's Thaw
Hope Springs
Summer Fling
Falling Softly

<u>Play Doctor</u>

Dream Machine
Healing Touch

STANDALONES
4-Ever Theirs
Nice & Naughty
Where There's Smoke
Report For Booty

RACING FOR LOVE
Driven
Shifting Gears

RED LIGHT
Through My Window
Star
Can't Buy Love
Free For All

PARANORMALS
Picture Perfect
Reborn
PICK YOUR PLEASURES
Pick Your Pleasure
Pick Your Pleasure 2

DEDICATION

In memory of the horrendously ugly green Chevy Nova my cousin Kris really did drown in an irrigation ditch during a flood, and all the fun times we had jamming the four ELKK club members onto the front bench seat for rides through the onion fields in our tiny New York hometown before that fateful day.

CHAPTER ONE

"Five hundred channels and there isn't shit on TV." Kaige Davis tossed the remote onto the leather sectional beside him. By early afternoon the Hot Rods' lazy Sunday had gotten *too* relaxed for his liking. Sitting on his ass this long at one stretch drove him beyond chilled out straight to Antsy Town. Maybe he'd see who else wanted to shoot some hoops or sketch designs for the skatepark they planned to install at the youth center.

Anything to get rid of this nervous energy.

"I'll take *Breaking Bad* reruns over having to sit through wedding junk any day." Holden scratched his chest beneath his vintage, if a little worn, Six Pak T-shirt. It was his favorite next to his faded Hooker Headers polo. None of them had bothered to change out of the clothes they'd slept in. "Sally keeps saying she wants something simple. If that's the case, what the hell do they need a planner for?"

"Pretty sure most people take longer than two months to organize their big day." Carver snorted. "They've got to get a cake, rent a tent and chairs and shit for the lawn, find someone really open-minded to officiate since the three of them can't formally get hitched. Then there's music. Plus, Sally needs a dress and we're probably going to have to wear tuxes. Or suits, at least."

"Don't fucking remind me," Bryce snarled. The man hated anything to do with pomp. He acted like he had a lethal allergy to formality.

"While we're waiting for them to come home, we could snag that new first-person shooter Alanso's been talking about. Maybe some pizzas too." Even Roman didn't seem excited by the idea, despite his legendary love for violent videogames. If Kaige didn't know better, he'd assume the guy had been some kind of commando—precise, cold and vicious when necessary. Both in their cartoon battles and in life. "If we practice, we could shrink wrap it downstairs before he gets home, act like we waited for him, then crush him and pretend he just sucks at it."

That would be kinda funny considering how Al, the douchecanoe, always wiped the floor with them. None of the five Hot Rods left in their shared apartment budged from the couch to instigate the prank, though.

They'd all busted ass lately, leaving them pretty zombified. Business had freaking exploded. Rave reviews spread by word of mouth at this season's car shows, seducing new clients by the truckload. At the same time, Eli, Alanso and Sally were understandably distracted. Interested in finding out what was under each other's hoods more than completing their projects in the shop.

How many times a day could they get it on with each other?

They had to have set a world record sometime in the past two months.

The combination of more to do with fewer helping hands had meant long hours for Kaige and the other unattached guys. Not that they minded. They loved what they did for a living—restoring badass classic cars—and no one could be happier for their googly-eyed friends. But lately they hadn't arranged any of their usual outings to blow off steam. Fishing trips, bar hopping and flaunting their restomod babies on long drives through curvy country roads had gotten slashed from their communal to-do list.

Especially since having fun at home in the evenings had sapped the last of their energy. Because unlike some couples, Eli, Alanso and Sally were into sharing.

Kaige had discovered he was too. The high he got from bonding even tighter with his friends blew him away. As addictive as crack, or maybe more, the passion they shared—not just for Hot Rods, but also for each other—never got old.

He might have assumed their wild sexathons would have burned out by now, lost some of the edge of those first taboo gatherings. Instead, it seemed the more comfortable they became, the better sexy stuff was between them. And no one was turning down another helping of their unique loving. At least they hadn't yet.

As if he could read Kaige's mind, or maybe he spotted the chubby starting to tent Super Nova's sweats, Roman spoke up.

"You know, there's one thing that never gets boring around here." He shifted his junk. "Too bad Cobra's going to be tasting cake for who knows how much longer. Could be the whole damn day if we're unlucky."

"Maybe this would be a good time for you to pony up on our bet, loser." Kaige rubbed his half-hard cock, which perked instantly at the prospect of a warm mouth massaging its growing length.

Damn, now that scheme had some merit.

Sure, the seven misfit mechanics and their one lone female grease monkey had been getting it on together pretty regularly since Eli and Alanso had staked their lifelong claim on Mustang Sally. Problem was, they'd been kind of stuck in neutral. Sally made it easy for them to drop their guard and justify the group action as some kind of glorified gangbang with her at the center of all their attention.

Kaige didn't mind admitting, at least to himself, that the intense demonstrations also reaffirmed the connection between the guys who'd become closer than brothers during the dark years of their adolescence. They'd found another way to commit to each other after nearly a decade of building a brighter future together.

All of them had waltzed into the youth center, originally run by Eli's mom, as teenagers. Chance had brought them together. Fate, maybe. Because they'd been able to help Eli puzzle together the jagged pieces of his own shattered life after his mother succumbed to an untimely illness. Following her death, Eli's dad—Tom—had taken over a big role as a mentor and leader in the community.

As if they were strays, he'd collected a bunch of the kids who needed homes and who fit into their motley pseudo-family until his heart brimmed with enough affection to mask his own staggering pain at the loss of his soul mate. Through the years, they'd helped each other survive some serious gloom, since they all could relate to the individual demons haunting them. Alanso's fear of abandonment. Eli's phobia of losing loved ones. Mustang Sally's way of always questioning group decisions to make sure they weren't brainwashing her like the sect of religious fanatics she'd escaped. Kaige's temper.

They battled their issues together.

Kaige had never felt more alive or accepted—part of something permanent—as when they got it on like a pack of wolves, which prized and guarded their mates.

It reaffirmed everything he clung to when the world felt uncertain.

Greedy, he wanted more from his partners—more honesty, more commitment and more passion. Without hiding behind Sally. Because someday, maybe he'd find a forever lady of his own...

Then what?

They had to accept Sally wasn't the glue binding them all together. It was more than that. Refusing to acknowledge the big picture was a disservice to the five guys in this room, who might hope for a partner of their own in addition to the chaotic releases they'd granted each other in their recent arrangement. Eli's cousin Joe and his Powertools Crew—a group of construction workers with a similar bond—promised it was possible.

If they could find women willing to sign up for a free-for-all of epic proportions...

First things first, though.

It was time to evolve again.

Kaige cracked his knuckles.

Carver glanced up from the auto magazine he'd been flipping through when he sensed Kaige's challenge. His raised brow signaled at least some interest in taking their discussion further, beyond trash talk. Bryce and Holden hadn't blinked yet. They sat in the corners of the sofa, all interest in the TV long since vanished.

"Come on, Barracuda. You welching?" Kaige leaned forward, planting his elbows on his knees as he took measure of their oldest roommate. Roman had lived out on the streets longest—survived alone, steeled himself against reality.

While hard knocks had tempered him, made him as undentable on the outside as a vintage stainless-steel bumper, it'd also left him the most broken on the inside. At least that was Kaige's theory.

Carver roomed with the guy. He'd volunteered to double up since their apartments had already been built by the time Roman joined them—after Tom had busted the guy trying to steal his truck and gave him an honest job at the fueling station attached to the garage downstairs instead of calling the cops.

The shorter, wiry Hot Rod may not have appeared as strong as his bunkmate, but he often eased the way for Barracuda in confrontational situations. Today was no exception.

Roman wiped a bead of sweat from his forehead with his knuckles despite the AC pumping an arctic breeze through their loft. Well, too damn bad. If he had a problem with blowing a dude, he shouldn't have run his mouth. He'd wagered a hummer that he could last longer than Kaige could while fucking Mustang Sally on their maiden voyage as a group. Underestimating the lure of her sweet pussy had been his downfall. To be fair, Kaige had only lasted a few seconds longer. Enough to secure the win.

Sex with Sally topped anything he'd done with barflies. It meant more, felt better, because the release it gifted him went beyond simple physical relief.

But Mustang was busy being girly for once, and he was horny. So this would have to do.

Besides, making Roman squirm wasn't easy. If nothing else, Kaige would enjoy having him hooked for a bit. If he really didn't get off on it though, Super Nova wouldn't force the guy.

What fun would that be?

Carver nudged Barracuda's knee with his own. "I've got this. You can detail my Road Runner for me later, okay?"

"Meep, you don't have to do it." Roman called his best friend by his nickname. They'd all adopted one based on their favorite cars. Sure, they'd worked on thousands at this point, but each Hot Rod had one they claimed as their baby. Carver's Plymouth Road Runner had earned him Meep. As in *meep meep*. He was a fast fucker when he needed to be. Sometimes, in those early days, Barracuda's lingering bad habits and runaway mouth when sloshed had gotten them in some tight situations.

"Hell, I'd much rather go down on Super Nova than slave over that beast in this heat." Carver slapped Roman on the back then rose from the couch, coming to stand in front of Kaige.

The twinkle in his hazel eyes wasn't uncommon, though it'd never been focused on Kaige quite like *that* before when the guy shrugged and declared, "I used to be pretty good at this. Enough to haul in some cash for food. It probably won't take more than ninety seconds to polish his knob. You'll be buffing chrome in the fucking sun for hours. Your loss, not mine."

Holden snorted. "That's probably a true story, all the way around."

"Yeah. I'm guessing it's not going to be a drawn-out affair." Bryce guffawed along with his buddy. None of them seemed fazed by Carver's confession. Neither would they judge him. They'd all done some unsavory things to survive before the Londons took them in. Bringing someone to orgasm was the least of their collective sins. They'd stand by Carver no matter what he'd had to do to make it.

"You'll be shooting into your own damn hands while I'm buried in a hot, wet mouth." Kaige shrugged. "Laugh all you want, boys. You're just jealous."

"Damn well better be." Carver tapped his jaw. "I may be rusty, but I demanded top dollar back in the day."

"Why don't you put your mouth where your money was?" Kaige lifted his ass high enough to swipe his elastic-waist pants to the tops of his thighs. He reached for his cock.

Carver beat him to it.

A surprised gurgle flew from his parted lips when his friend skillfully manhandled his junk as if it were the shifter of his beloved ride. Without hesitation, Meep fished Kaige's half-hard tool out and aimed it toward his open, descending mouth.

The guy shoved Kaige's thighs wider than he was used to spreading them in order to accommodate the slender shoulders of a woman. His groin protested until Meep made him forget all about the minor discomfort.

Super Nova shivered as Carver's breath washed over his sac and the base of his erection. Of course he'd seen Alanso hoover Eli a bunch of times these past months. Those visuals hadn't prepared him for what it would feel like to have another dude's hands on him.

Rough calluses rubbed him as Carver's fingers surrounded him, more comfortably accommodating Kaige's girth than any girlfriend had ever managed. Not that he was huge or anything, but he made a nice handful for his friend. "Shit!"

"Too hard?" The single raised brow on Meep's face spoke more of taunt than genuine concern. Kaige didn't give a fuck. Let him tease all he wanted, as long as he sealed those lips he licked over Kaige's raging hard-on sometime this century.

"You tell me." Super Nova rocked his hips upward, thrusting his cock through the ring of his friend's fingers.

"Nah. You feel great." Carver smiled then flicked his tongue out before Kaige could brace himself for the initial contact. "Taste good too."

"Fuck, that's hot," Bryce growled. Kaige caught motion in his peripheral vision and took half a second to check it out. Sure enough, their Rebel nearly tore his boxers in his haste to reach his own monster stiffy.

Not to be left in their dust, Roman and Holden did the same. Soon the three guys in their audience paced themselves, stroking in sync to the tempo Carver set with sure, solid passes of his fist on Kaige.

"Too much more of that and I won't make it to the main event," he warned Meep in a rasp so husky he might have blushed, if he were capable of such a thing after so much rough living.

"We're only getting started. Don't ruin everyone's fun so soon." Carver squeezed the base of Kaige's shaft, pressing solidly in exactly the right spot to grant him a reprieve from his trek to cloud nine. "Besides, if I don't blow you, then I suppose the bet isn't paid up and we'll have to start all over again."

"Yeah, Super Nova. Exploding prematurely isn't allowed." Roman spoke up for his best friend—the guy who'd willingly knelt in his place. "Let Meep enjoy his treat. Help him forget about *having* to do this and make him remember *wanting* to instead."

Well, shit. When Barracuda put it like that, Kaige would be glad to perform this community service. As often as necessary to obliterate another ghost from their pasts. Purely selfless. Yeah, sure. But that was how things worked with the Hot Rods. They healed each other simply by being together. They'd been doing it for over a decade.

He looked up, absorbing the force of his friends' attention. Their stares riveted on the intersection of his body and Carver's. The other guy had progressed, now fitting his mouth over the weeping head of Kaige's cock. He slurped the puddle on top before gliding effortlessly to the base, in one long move.

Jesus.

As if that weren't enough to redline Super Nova's engine and nearly blast the top of his skull off, having his friends witness his surrender to Carver's unbelievable fucking hotness only fueled his revving.

Kaige groaned again, thinking of all the times they'd watched pornos and jerked off together. Somehow having their interest lasering in on him—instead of some actress or three with enormous fake tits—felt completely different.

Intense and sort of sacred.

He shook his head hard enough that his dreads came loose from the black leather tie he'd captured them in. They slapped against his brightly tattooed shoulders. The brushing contact had him wishing the Hot Rods were all gathered tight around him. Petting him like they'd done to Mustang Sally these past months, coddling her when she proved brave enough to submit to their combined affections.

He wanted them to approve of him using Meep so well. Or was it the other way around?

For now, he'd settle for ogling his friends right back. Maybe even goading them with extra-loud moans of approval when Carver eased up on the suction to lick and nip the underside of Kaige's shaft.

"You realize you three could give each other a hand and make that more fun, don't you?" Carver didn't pause his manipulation of Kaige's throbbing cock when he joined the mischief-making efforts. He simply transferred the motion to his deft fingers so he could peek over at their buddies, as if daring them to stay separate when he had been bold enough to cross this bridge.

Bryce and Holden exchanged a glance then shrugged. They fisted each other's shafts. Both of them cried out at the contact of another guy's flesh pressed to their own. Off to the side—alone—Roman nearly tore his cock off with savage yanks as he studied his roommate devouring Kaige.

Super Nova had sensed that Barracuda preferred his sex extreme, like most other aspects of his life—drinking, gambling and racing. Although he'd maintained an iron grip on his control when he fucked Sally, he seemed a little less enthused than the rest of them during their group sessions, which had remained pretty vanilla...

If you didn't count that whole seven-guys-on-one-girl action thing.

Still, Roman had never hesitated to plow her. He'd emptied himself just as vigorously as the rest of them into the condoms they all had agreed without discussion to wear when they played with her. No doubt she belonged primarily to Eli and Alanso.

If they ever wanted to start a family, well, that was up to them.

"Hang on." Kaige tapped Carver's cheek as he realized what they'd unwittingly done in their eagerness. His erection flagged the teeniest bit. "I should have gotten protection for you. I think there are some mint rubbers in the stash. I'm clean, don't worry, but I know we usually..."

"Shut up." Meep smacked Kaige's inner thigh, spreading warmth and the flare of sweet pleasurable pain through his nervous system. Barracuda grunted in response, as if ready to beg his roomie to do it again. "Things are different with Sally. No chances. I'm safe, and I know you are too, right?"

"Of course. I never would have put you at risk if..." It was hard to think when Meep rededicated himself to sucking Kaige's cock as if he were trying to drink the come straight out of Kaige's balls.

Nova grabbed the edges of the leather cushion he sat on, crushing it in his grip as he wrestled his libido for the power to endure. It felt too good to let this end so quickly.

Roman chuckled from his perch on the peninsula portion of the sectional. "You're doing a damn fine job, boy. Keep sucking. Harder. He likes it when you take him into your throat like that."

Kaige let his head drop back, exposing his neck to the only men he trusted not to rip it out. He couldn't watch anymore.

A hum buzzed the length of his dick, now fully embedded in Carver's mouth. The guy began to swallow around him, undulating his tongue against the underside of Kaige's shaft in a come-hither motion.

Engrossed in the pure ecstasy his friend delivered, Kaige didn't register the clang caused by three people clomping up the metal stairway outside their apartment. Not until the door swung open and his sluggish mind belatedly processed the input.

"Honeys, we're home!" Alanso shouted as he practically skipped inside after a day of plotting the ceremony that would seal his trio's happily ever after. "Did you miss—?"

He cut off when he realized what they were up to inside.

"I guess that's a no." Eli London, the shop's owner—their King Cobra—nearly bowled over his soon-to-be husband as he shoved them across the threshold.

Mustang Sally let out an *oomph* as she piled into Cobra, bringing up the rear. "What's going on? Why'd you slam on the brakes?"

She peeked around her pair of guys and stutter-stepped. "Oh. Awesome."

Then she was jogging toward them, sliding on her knees across the faux fur rug, ignoring the corner of the coffee table that jabbed her hip as she settled in for a front row seat.

"Want some help with that?" She rubbed Carver's shoulders, maybe knowing from experience how uncomfortable it could be to attend to one of the guys. Not that Meep would complain or stop, but Kaige appreciated her assistance since his overriding lust made it difficult to ensure their friend's experience remained positive.

The guarantee of comfort for their fellow Hot Rod was welcome, especially given his history. Nova hoped his wide smile conveyed what he couldn't vocalize.

Carver pulled off with a slurp that left Kaige about to whimper and beg for more.

"Nah." He slapped Kaige's cock against his swollen lips as he reassured Sally. "If Super Nova doesn't mind, I'd like to keep him to myself this time."

Sally kissed Meep's cheek. She slipped her hand up his nape and guided him back to Kaige's rock-hard shaft. "Then get busy so I can taste you afterward instead."

With the proper motivation, Carver worked double time. The guy slithered his tongue in patterns and places Kaige had never fathomed before. Meep skimmed Kaige's frenulum and the piercing through it before drawing lightly on the ring.

Pressure there always had him toeing the edge in an instant.

It didn't help that Eli and Alanso had joined Bryce and Holden on the couch, directly across from where Carver attempted to suck Kaige's brains out. Cobra had already extracted his cock and helped Alanso do the same. The bald guy crashed against the cushions when his lover took possession of his hard-on and matched his rhythm to the one they all fell in step with—whether being jerked or blown.

"That's it. You're doing such a good job," Sally purred to Carver even as she squeezed Kaige's knee. Knowing she didn't object and that she wasn't repulsed by their demonstration of base arousal was the last push he needed.

His balls drew tight. He attempted to caution Carver. The warning wouldn't form as anything more coherent than an endless stream of moans and sighs, which escaped his parted lips at the decadent treatment by his friend.

Sally helped him out. "He's ready, Meep. Take him all the way. Swallow him. Drain him."

Dirty talk did it for Kaige. Always had.

His fingers went from fisted in the cushion to splayed outward in rigid spikes that would put a porcupine to shame. Frozen, his entire body strained to the max.

He hung in midair for what seemed like forever.

Then his cock caught up with his brain. It flexed in time to the blasts of his come, which launched from his balls into Meep's hungry mouth.

The man couldn't quite keep up. A pearl of come appeared at the corner of his mouth before he reapplied himself to his mission.

Super Nova stayed true to his nickname, pouring himself down his friend's throat in explosive bursts. He grabbed Carver's arm and held on so he wouldn't launch into orbit. Meanwhile, his other hand was sandwiched by Sally's two smaller, softer ones. They anchored him tenderly as his world flew apart.

And when he thought he couldn't spasm even one more time without dropping dead, Bryce and Holden joined him almost simultaneously. Pearly strands shot from their cocks and made a mess of their chiseled abs, not to mention their fingers. Roman was only a millisecond behind. He never took his eyes from the red ring of Carver's lips, which surrounded Kaige's still-pulsing cock, as he spilled his seed in an impressive arc.

Meep cared for Kaige, letting him down slowly. Only once Kaige had softened considerably did Carver surrender his grip and nuzzle Sally.

"How's that?" He licked his lips as if he'd enjoyed the taste of Kaige's come as much as the s'mores ice cream he stashed in the freezer for dessert—one scoop every night. The possibility had another droplet leaking from Super Nova's tip. Quick to swipe his thumb over Kaige's ultrasensitive head, Meep harvested that last bit as enthusiastically as he lapped melted dregs from his bowl when he thought no one was looking.

"Debt paid. In full." Kaige gasped his praise. Then he ruffled the other Hot Rod's already mussed hair before shoving him away. It was either that or start to get hard again. He wasn't sure he was ready to declare so boldly that he'd loved his friend's attention.

Late to the party, Eli and Alanso were warmed up enough to claim their lady.

"Come here, Sally," Cobra ordered.

"But what about Meep?" She helped their friend rise onto the couch where he caught his breath and stretched his legs.

"I've got him." Roman surprised them as he shooed Sally toward her lovers.

Eli and Alanso welcomed her between them. Quickly, they stripped off her cargo capris then bent her so that she could accept Eli's long cock in her pussy. Without direction, she took Alanso in her mouth as if they'd been practicing sexual gymnastics forever.

A second round of lusty play began when Roman towered over Carver. Under the Hot Rods' careful observation, his stony façade melted, leaving behind a lava-hot passion

Kaige had never spied in their friend's eyes before.

"Get those pants off. Now." Barracuda didn't mess around when he pointed at Meep's ripped denim. Though the guy's jutting cock made it tricky, he divested himself of the skinny jeans pretty damn quick. Mostly, anyway, though the pants hung from his ankle where he hadn't quite kicked them free.

Kaige tried to recover enough to facilitate the process, but his muscles were completely liquefied.

Barracuda flashed his pearly-white teeth as he grabbed the leg of Carver's jeans and yanked, stripping his roommate in a flash. He shoved his way between Meep's thighs on the couch and ground their hips together.

The sticky mess Roman had made on his own belly transferred to Carver. "Did you see what you did to me? Can you feel it?"

"Uh." Meep seemed dazed. "Yeah."

"Next time it'll be *me* that you drink." Barracuda shocked them all by biting Carver's neck hard enough to leave a mark.

Holy shit.

Meep shuddered beneath his friend, certainly not from pain.

"Now show me what you've got." Roman lifted up enough to jam his fist between them.

He measured the length of Carver's cock with uneven jerks. The purple tip poked from the top rung of Barracuda's fingers before he reversed the gesture, his hand rising up to squeeze the head. He milked their friend like a pro.

Kaige supposed it wasn't so different from masturbating, really.

Except it was.

Sally shattered the temporary stillness with a cry Kaige had come to recognize as an accompaniment to her orgasm. The clench of her pussy must have wrung a climax from Eli too. He roared as he filled her. The sight of their rapture lured Alanso into joining his forever partners.

"Are you pleased with what you've done? To them all, boy?" Roman showed no mercy as he pumped Carver faster and faster. "Give us the same satisfaction. Let us watch you come apart."

The strained whine Meep surrendered had Kaige reaching out to surround the guy's ankle with his closest hand. Why was Roman being so hard on him? Refusing to grant even a bit of kindness? And why did Carver seem to respond so earnestly to that mistreatment?

Did he like being bossed around? Or was he conditioned to react to authority from his days on the street?

As if the mean cant cracked Barracuda's heart too—if the guy even had that organ beating in his cold chest—he leaned down and shocked them all. Carver especially, if his keening whimper could be entered as evidence.

Roman kissed Carver. Full on the mouth.

The instant their lips touched, Meep went wild. He twitched as if he were being jolted by a lightning bolt or a live wire as he sprayed his come across Barracuda's torso. A particularly powerful spurt tagged Roman's neck.

Kaige's limp cock twitched at the demonstration of unadulterated lust.

How the hell had they kept that bottled inside?

Why had they?

He didn't give a shit as long as it was out in the open now. Because no way could they shove it back into the shadows and pretend tonight had never happened.

Even if they'd wanted to, Eli would never allow it. Not after the pain he'd caused Alanso by doing the same, shrouding the bond between them until it had almost severed. They'd learned that lesson the hard way.

Relief—both physical and something less concrete—radiated through Kaige.

For the first time in months he felt rested.

Gradually, the guys became aware of their surroundings. They cleaned up and joked about the epic release they'd shared. Things were maybe a little weird, but less so than when they'd been lying to themselves about what their unusual bond really entailed.

Five minutes or so had passed when side conversations developed. Alanso and Sally shared the details they'd worked out about their commitment ceremony.

Eli surprised Kaige by crossing to sit next to him. He appreciated the company from the bossman since Roman and Carver seemed to be holding their own congress next door to Nova. Their link had always been tighter, and he didn't want to intrude.

"I leave you alone for one fucking afternoon and look what happens." Cobra slapped a hand on Kaige's thigh and squeezed. "If I'd known that's what would go down, I'd have done it weeks ago."

Kaige huffed. "Hey, just claiming my winnings from the bet."

"Whatever it takes, man." Eli grinned before turning serious. "I hope you know how much I appreciate all your help lately. Here at home *and* in running the shop. Since this went down…"

"No problem." He knocked his shoulder into King Cobra's. "It's about time you trusted me to back you up. Plus I've gotten a chance to put some of my ideas in place for the business."

"I've always tr—"

Kaige waved him off. "I know. But you were too anal to let go until Alanso loosened that tight ass of yours."

"I guess I can't deny that." Eli laughed. "But I'm a different guy now. So when I saw an opportunity today, I took it. You up for an early meeting in the morning?"

"Sure." Opening the garage had become Kaige's responsibility lately. He didn't mind at all. "What's going on?"

"The wedding planner…" Eli's halting explanation tolled a warning bell in the base of Kaige's spine. "She's part of a consulting business with her sister. Ms. Brown was there too and gave me her card. I took one look and knew she could get us on track with the extra prospects we're missing lately."

"What?" Kaige glared at Cobra. "Nothing's slipping through the cracks. I made sure of it."

"That's not what I mean, Super Nova." Eli held his hands out, palms facing Kaige. "There's a lot happening. I'm not sure we're giving each opportunity our full attention like we should. Ms. Brown will help us make sure we capitalize on the new avenues opening for us. Let's hear her out, okay? If she's half as good at business management as her sister is at coordinating events, we're going to be golden."

"Did I fuck something up? Why wouldn't you have the balls to tell me?" Kaige bolted to his feet, whipping his pants around his waist. Suddenly, having his junk dangling around this guy didn't feel safe in the least.

How dare Cobra act like Kaige hadn't spent weeks formulating a strategy for moving forward because he hadn't been around to hear it mapped out?

"Huh?" Eli tilted his head slightly. "No. Shit, Nova. You've done great. I just thought we could use some help. I can tell you're tired. All of us are. Ms. Brown really impressed me today. I bet she'll be able to get things under control a bit. Maybe find some more efficient processes to ease the load on everybody."

"And you didn't even think about discussing this with me before you hired an outsider to come dip her fingers in my pie?" Kaige tried to stop the red tide washing over his vision.

It was too late.

He had to escape before he blew. Notorious for his temper, he'd tried desperately to tame the rage that sometimes overtook him.

Right now he was failing. Like he hadn't in years. Refusing to give Cobra or the rest of the guys the satisfaction of seeing him flip his shit, Kaige stormed toward the door.

"What the fuck, Super Nova?" Eli started to rise. Alanso and Sally took his hands and kept him from following. They knew continuing down this road would only result in an assortment of black eyes between them.

"Let him cool off," Mustang Sally counseled her man. To his credit, he actually listened.

Maybe he wasn't a total dumbass after all. Maybe their deepening relationships had changed them each for the better.

But if that was true, maybe Kaige *had* dropped the ball.

Failing the Hot Rods was the last thing he wanted to do.

Sick and barefoot, he jogged down the spiky stairs and across the driveway, out of sight from their apartment, without a care for the rocks jabbing his soles or the pain radiating up his calves.

It took away from the bruises on his heart.

Damn them.

The hurt only enraged him further.

He'd sworn never to let anyone have the power to make him vulnerable again.

Too late.

CHAPTER TWO

Kaige roared as he kicked a stack of bald tires waiting behind their storage shed to be recycled. He probably broke his bare toe. Certainly he screwed up Holden's tidy arrangements. None of that mattered when rage consumed him. A red haze tinted his vision, and he imagined himself as one of the berserkers that had sprouted a branch of his family tree. His blond hair and blue eyes declared him part Viking at least, though he'd traded the war braids of his ancestors for dreadlocks.

Hauling back, he loosed another volley of roundhouses and punches on the unyielding rubber. Dissatisfied with his progress in destroying the neat columns, he hoisted one of the heavy rings and chucked it a solid fifteen feet. It smashed into a giant oak tree and bounced before rolling away in a wobbly path that made it look drunk off its ass. Barked profanity accompanied its flight.

None of his childish responses eased the sense of failure shredding his insides. It never did. He should know by this point in his life that frothing at the mouth only transformed him into a younger version of his fanatical father.

Genetics were a bitch to combat.

Hell, he'd be thirty this year. Yet he still hadn't tamed the beast inside him. The part of him he loathed. Worst of all, he got more steamed because this bullshit hissy fit had destroyed the calm following his killer orgasm. Sweaty sex was one of the few remedies he'd found to successfully leech his anger. His connection with the Hot Rods had been another.

Apparently not today. On either count.

"Fuck! Fuck! Fuck!" A curse accompanied each pummel of his fist, which clipped a valve stem on one of his passes through the late-afternoon shadows. They cast long blobs across this side of the property. Shit, that stung. Warm blood trickled over his knuckles, reminding him of days when fuckwad punks had given him something more satisfactory to beat. Like the bully—a fellow homeless teen—who had harassed him endlessly. The kid had finally filched the ratty box and newspaper bedding Kaige had slept in beneath the bridge he'd called home for a few years. It hadn't been the first of his meager possessions the jerk had stolen rather than share, despite Kaige's gracious offers.

It had been the last, though.

What he wouldn't give for a good fight right now. Instead, he continued to mangle his fists on the inanimate objects he painted with a dozen different faces. Stopping and holding on the bastard he'd escaped. A piss-poor excuse for a sire. Because nearly freezing to death, starving, defending himself against pervs—not to mention older, crazier people than him on the street—and relying on the swish of endless cars flying across the highway overpass above his shelter to lull him to sleep had been better than hanging around in that damned house after his mother had "disappeared".

Like every time he unleashed his animal side, he wanted nothing more than to pound the dickface, probably-murdering father who'd regularly behaved...exactly like Kaige was acting right now.

Shame slumped his shoulders. Steam poured off of him, wilting his entire frame.

Breathing hard, he stared at the bright red spatters mixing with sweat before trailing down his torso and wrists like bloody tears. Was this what his dad had looked like after he killed Kaige's mother and got away with murder because no one gave a fuck except a helpless brat?

Most likely.

Except worse. Way worse.

Could he ever snap, like he had today, and hurt someone besides himself? Someone he cared about?

He hoped not, but...

Fuck.

"You almost burned out, kid?" Tom's soft question didn't disguise his concern well enough. "Thought you had that temper under control these days."

"I'm out here, aren't I?" he snarled, despite his best attempt at staying calm. Biting the hand that fed him all those years ago wasn't his intention. "Beating the shit out of some old tires instead of your hardheaded son."

"In that case, I'm glad you're venting on these poor Goodyears." Tom chuckled until Kaige spun to face him, intending to jog past and grab his keys. A ride would finish clearing his head.

"Jesus!" Eli's father by birth, dad to all of the Hot Rods by choice, reached out when he spotted the damage Kaige had done to himself. "Come on, Nova. Let me clean you up."

"I'm not fifteen anymore. It's not like I scraped my knee or some shit." Kaige shrugged and dodged, afraid of contact with any decent human being. He felt dirty, and not because of the iron tang building in the air.

"Like you would have let me nurse that either." Tom rolled his eyes.

"When'd you become such a mother hen?" He tried to distance himself again.

"Right about the time my wife died and left me alone with a young son...seven sons and a daughter, though I didn't know it then...to raise on my own." No matter how much time passed, Mr. London had never fully recovered from losing the love of his life. Their screwed-up system had worked in part because he was every bit as mangled inside as the kids he'd sheltered.

"Shit, Tom. I'm sorry." Although he congratulated himself on keeping his tone level, inside he seethed. Because again he'd hurt someone he respected. He couldn't do anything right, it seemed.

"It's okay." Tom kept convincing him with that utterly placid stare and his steady grip, which led Kaige toward Tom's neat house halfway between the garage and the shed. He must have spotted Kaige bolting past. Instead of taking him inside, he escorted his charge to the garden behind his home.

They sat together near the memorial markers Sally had made in honor of the mothers both Eli and Alanso had lost. Maybe he could ask her to paint one for his mom too someday. When it didn't hurt so much to think about it. Another decade might do the trick.

Kaige crashed onto the bench nearby. Tom paused to dip his handkerchief in the stream that meandered around the seating area before joining him. He handed Kaige the cool, damp, folded cloth. "You're all right, Nova. Everyone's got their buttons. Which one did my son mash today?"

Kaige gritted his teeth as he wiped blood and sweat from his bare chest before rinsing out the soft cotton and wrapping the soothing square around his already swollen hand. After a minute of silence, he switched it to the other. He couldn't afford to lose mobility in his fingers with the Culverson job on the schedule for tomorrow. It'd be a lot of detail work installing the custom dash and gauges.

The fabrication of parts like these marked one direction he hoped to take the garage. Unique skills would go a long way in making Hot Rods the premiere customizer in the Midwest. The high profit margin on the work would ensure their success and allow them to subsidize divisions of the business they enjoyed, even if they weren't necessarily cash cows. It was a central pillar of his strategy. Maybe one he should have shared with Eli sooner. After all, if he had, the bossman might not have assumed Kaige was sleeping on the job. Too bad he hadn't wanted to burden Eli with details given his infatuation with Al and Sally lately.

Kaige's grimace had nothing to do with the sting of his shallow cuts and everything to do with King Cobra's mandated assistance. Realizing how long he and Tom had lingered there in silence, he wasn't sure if the older guy still wanted to know what had caused the ruckus. But at least the sounds of the trickling water and the orange flash of koi swimming past helped Kaige regain his composure.

Serenity. He needed some bad.

The clearing of his raw throat sounded harsh in the still evening. He returned to the bench and took a seat next to Tom.

"Eli thinks I did a shit job as second-in-command these past couple months." Nova let his head hang back so he could study the sky, which edged toward twilight.

"What?" Tom sat up fast enough to rock the bench. "No, he doesn't. He's told me several times how grateful he is for your help and that... Oh."

"*Oh*, what?" Kaige looked up enough to raise a brow at his real dad. The only one who'd ever counted for shit.

"He regrets the strain he's putting on you. On everyone. Did he try to reclaim some responsibility to lift the burden?" Stuck between Eli and Kaige, Tom would never take sides. He was fair and always had been. So it made it hard to dismiss his speculation out of hand.

"He hired a consultant before discussing it with me. Or anyone." Kaige sighed. "Some prissy old lady, *Ms. Brown*, who's going to show up tomorrow morning and tell us how she thinks we should run the joint."

"Ouch." Tom shook his head. "Eli should have spoken to you first."

Hating to defend the asshole, Kaige cleared his throat. "He said it was an impulse. She's the sister of the wedding planner."

"Ah, now we're getting somewhere." Tom nodded. "I believe my son can be hasty. Hell, all of you guys are."

"Learned that from the best." He smiled at his mentor. "Who else would offer up their own home to a runaway after only knowing him a few hours? Shit, seven times, for that matter."

"Sometimes you have to trust your gut." Tom held his hands up. "I'm not making excuses for Eli. He could have texted you or something on that phone of his that does everything but wipe his ass. You know, while he was at his appointment. But maybe you should meet Ms. Brown and give her a chance before you decide my son thinks less of you than I know he does."

Kaige took a deep breath and then another. The thought of someone snooping around in the work he'd done, judging his efforts, still didn't sit well. But what Tom said made sense. Damn him.

As anger ebbed and rationality returned, he allowed himself to consider things from Cobra's perspective. Could hiring help have been a misplaced gesture of kindness, or guilt?

Son of a bitch. Maybe.

But Kaige didn't have to like it.

"Thanks, Tom." He smirked as he met the guy's gaze dead-on for the first time. "I'll give it a try. I won't deck anybody, but I can't promise I won't be a pain in the ass."

"You wouldn't be the Super Nova I know and love if you could help yourself from that."

They laughed together.

"I bet you ten bucks Ms. Brown doesn't make it to lunchtime." Kaige grinned.

"Hmm. We'll see." Tom might have shook on their wager if Kaige's knuckles hadn't drawn a wince from the older guy. Instead he laid his hand on Nova's wrist and squeezed.

***

Kaige refused to groan as he trailed his aching fingers along the orange and yellow stitching that dotted the green leather inside his Nova. The colors exactly matched the flames running down the side panels of the emerald metallic paintjob Sally had slaved over. Holden had done a phenomenal job with the interior, attending to the tiniest details, like the constellations embroidered across the headrests. His friend always did great work. Still, this had to be some of his best. Anything they did for a fellow Hot Rod went above and beyond.

The wide bench seat made a great couch. Kaige reclined, with one arm behind his head and his feet crossed, ankles resting in the open window as he finished reading the news on his tablet. By getting up at the ass crack of dawn, he'd escaped to the garage to avoid crashing into any of the other members of their gang.

Childish and embarrassing, his outburst from the night before left a bad taste in his mouth. Bitter. He couldn't believe he'd lost his cool. Worse, he could only hope he could resign himself to freezing out Ms. Brown today with a chilly welcome, instead of caving to another bout of rage. Especially in light of everything that had come before his explosion. They hadn't gotten a chance to discuss what yesterday's fun meant for them going forward. Had it been a onetime show?

He didn't think so.

More like, he hoped not.

Lunchtime couldn't come soon enough. On his break he'd call up one of the Powertools crew members—Dave, maybe—and see what advice their more experienced counterparts had for him about bridging the gap between friend and lover now that he was calm enough to listen. Kaige planned to use the rest of the day sweating side-by-side, hard at work, with his friends. Manual labor in their garage bays should take the edge off any awkwardness. Tonight they could dive into details, and likely each other, again.

Damn it! Not now. He ignored the pulsing of his cock in his coveralls. Luckily the loose fabric would help disguise any untimely chubbies. The odds of an inappropriate hard-on reoccurrence, or a dozen, before dinner were pretty damn good. Unless Ms. Brown shriveled his balls permanently when they met up in...

Kaige glanced at the time displayed on the modified vintage radio—all the looks of a classic with the conveniences of a modern day ride. Perfect. Three minutes to go before he had to face the music.

He supposed he could have wandered into the office early, but that meant either loitering there like a kid waiting for the principal to arrive after he'd fucked up royally or making small talk with Cobra. Probably the later, since Eli usually refused to be anything but punctual. Unless Alanso or Sally distracted him, as they had more and more often recently.

Considering last night, Kaige figured it was best not to get riled up before the meeting.

For Tom, he'd try to keep an open mind. Assume King Cobra had positive intentions. Once he'd chased off the meddling Ms. Brown, he would have a chance to show his friend what tricks he'd been keeping up his sleeves for the future of the garage.

"Yo, Super Nova." Bryce startled Kaige when he passed the rolled-down window near his head. "Quit hiding and get to work."

"I'm not—"

"Sure. Get over your moping then." Rebel grinned as he joked, though the sting resulting from his jabs proved there might be some truth to his taunts. Kaige watched his friend through the front glass of his windshield as the guy set up his station. Bryce was their customer service rep in addition to a kickass mechanic. He had a way of keeping people calm and smoothing things over with a professionalism that Kaige envied. Today seemed to be no exception. "I saw your nine o'clock pulling up just now. And Eli's already in his office. Don't make him more grumpy by not starting on the dot."

"He's pissed at me?" Kaige couldn't necessarily blame Cobra. He'd robbed them of the chance to iron shit out in private before their audience with a stranger. If nothing else, Hot Rods stuck together.

"Nah. I think he's more annoyed with himself." The big guy rubbed the back of his neck with one hand. "I can see both sides. I think he realizes now that he should have approached the situation differently."

"Hey, don't worry." Super Nova flipped his tablet closed and gave his friend his full attention. Rebel hated when they fought between them. Maybe it was something from his past he'd never divulged. In fact, of all the Hot Rods, Kaige knew the least about Bryce's history. He'd always been super tight-lipped about his life before Hot Rods. Even more than Roman, and that was saying something.

"It's gonna be okay. We'll work it out. I promise."

"I know." Bryce smiled. "We always do. I don't like to see you two at each other's throats, that's all. Any of us, really. It's not worth it, you know. We've been through enough shit we had no control over to get tangled up in stuff we can do something about."

"I'm going. Right now." Kaige sat up and swung his feet out of the now-open door. He stepped into his boots and laced them up. While he did, he looked to Bryce and grinned. "We'll kiss and make up. No worries, Rebel."

"Get the hell out of here."

A leather work glove hit him in the head, scattering his dreads around his face, as he strutted toward the main office of the garage, still smiling.

They'd make it through today. Like every day.

Kaige shoved open the glass door separating the garage from the front office of the shop. He stepped inside and nearly tripped over the mat designed to keep the low pile, industrial carpets reasonably free of oil and dirt.

Ms. Brown perched on the edge of a molded plastic guest chair across the wide desk from Eli, who sprawled in his King Cobra throne, fashioned from the seat of a Ferrari F360 Challenge. Her spine risked cracking from being forced so straight and her long, graceful fingers were folded in her lap.

Kaige blinked then looked back and forth between the shop owner and the consultant the guy had hired on sight yesterday. Now this was starting to make more sense. After all, Super Nova took one glance at her and knew what he'd like to do.

Though nailing her up against the wall really had nothing to do with work and everything to do with leisure.

Rich mocha skin and wide brown eyes offset the pearly white of her teeth. Seriously kissable lips were enhanced by a deep maroon gloss. Lustrous hair in oversized waves curled below her shoulders, making him dream about tugging it just a little as he slid inside her over and over.

He shook his head to clear it. Unsuccessfully.

This beautiful young woman was no *Ms. Brown*. Hell no, she could try to hide behind that prim and proper suit jacket all she wanted. It didn't obscure her lush breasts or the tiny waist that flared to perfectly curved hips. At most, he put her in her mid-twenties.

Right in range…

He was screwed. How could he freeze out someone who warmed him instantly? Shaking his head, he dedicated himself to doing exactly that.

***

"Kaige Davis, this is Ms. Brown. Her sister feels confident about pulling off the wedding in the next two weeks, like Sally hoped. Ms. Brown thought she could lend a hand on the business side of things to keep me freed up to help on the matrimonial front." Eli couldn't have phrased his introduction more politically. What was he hinting at?

Nola Brown squinted at the two men facing off, wondering if the office would get torn to shreds if the menacing newcomer decided to revolt. Why wouldn't he stop glaring at her?

As if one surly bastard would scare her off? He had no idea the places she'd come from. Instead of wilting beneath his stare, which lingered too long on the curve of her breasts to be completely impartial, she sat straighter and snuffed the urge to adjust her suit jacket. She also refused to think about how damn attractive his sullen blue eyes, blond dreads and tattooed muscles were.

Dear Lord, did he have to flash that colorful art beneath his loose coveralls, which didn't do a damn thing to disguise his trim work-enhanced body?

She focused on what the sexy garage owner had said, every clue a tool to use in securing his business. An account like this on her resume would do a lot of good.

So this had more to do with the burden of the wedding than his shop manager's lack of strategic goals, huh?

Jotting a mental note, she resolved to ask his opinions once they got started. An ally would go a long way in making her job a success. Unfortunately his grimace didn't make it seem as if he wanted to be pals.

"What's your name?" The hostility in Kaige's tone stole her voice for a moment.

Luckily, Eli covered for her. "I already introduced you to Ms. Brown."

The guy who insisted on being called Cobra spoke slowly, as if Kaige were dense or maybe as if he feared offending the asshole who was supposed to be his friend.

When she'd met the tough garage owner and his tougher lovers the day before yesterday, she never imagined the rest of the Hot Rods would make those three look like gentle ambassadors. Nola dug deep and extracted the front she'd worn as a youth on the streets.

She stood, towering in her six-inch heels, and jammed out her hand. "Nola, Nola Brown."

Without hesitation, he returned the clutch with interest, while she wondered at the crinkle blossoming around the corners of his eyes—yeah, she'd tried to make him uncomfortable, but a guy like him shouldn't dent beneath even her firmest grip—for a moment before glancing down and catching sight of scabbed knuckles. Who had he pummeled?

Banged-up hands but not a bruise on that pretty face meant it had been no contest.

For an eternity, they locked horns—or hands—their gazes clashing as if they indulged in a world-record-setting staring contest. Neither of them volunteered to back down first.

Until Eli intervened with a less-than-subtle clearing of his throat.

Balancing her no-nonsense stance with Kaige and the necessity of pleasing his boss, she yanked free of the newcomer's hold, trying to convince herself that the pulse hammering through her veins had more to do with annoyance than attraction.

Because that was a really, really bad idea.

"I was talking to the lady." Kaige flumped into the seat beside the one she'd recently occupied and slouched, his long legs stretching all the way to the base of the desk in front of him.

"Looked more like a pissing contest to me." Eli grinned.

He waved her off when she began to give some lame excuse for their immature showdown. "He deserved it. You don't have to spare anyone's feelings around here. We're big boys and girls. Or should be. Guess you see why we call him Super Nova, though. He's got a bit of a temper. Sorry 'bout that."

Nola nodded. "No worries. I can handle myself."

"Nobody doubts that, honey." The lascivious slant to Super Nova's glance had her insides squirming despite her no-fucking-way chastising. She'd long ago trained herself to ignore bad boys. They only brought trouble.

Somehow, she knew that went double for this one.

She cleared her throat. "So tell me what you're looking for? Why am I here?"

"Am I allowed to make suggestions?" Nova winked.

"No," Nola and Eli responded in unison.

Eli, King Cobra, repeated his spiel from their initial meeting about generating a long-term strategy, organizing existing ideas and formalizing their business plan, which they both understood was for the benefit of Kaige, not her.

She hoped the toolbox was listening. He seemed more intent on playing games, leaving his legs spread so his knee maintained contact with hers. If he thought she'd head for the hills before they even got started, he was destined for disappointment. Intimidation tactics had never worked on her.

"Excuse me." She stopped Eli mid-sentence and turned to face the asshole beside her instead. "I don't give a shit how big you think your balls are, you don't need all that room. Move the hell over. This is my space."

She drew an imaginary box around herself, uninviting Kaige from within it.

Nola didn't bother to glance away from Nova's stunned expression toward the gasping Eli didn't come close to covering with his faux cough. Thank God he busted a gut at her directness instead of booting her to the curb. Maybe this could work after all.

Kaige shuffled to the left then splayed his legs even wider than before. She didn't give a fuck as long as he kept away from her. Turing toward Eli again, she caught his stare in her peripheral vision. She wondered if the glimmer there had anything to do with begrudging respect, or if resentment still took top spot.

She didn't come here today to make enemies. And whether she'd asked for it or not, she had one. The only way to get this job, and keep it, would be to form an unlikely alliance.

Fuck her life.

"I think what you're saying makes sense, Cobra." She felt silly using their nicknames but the guys wore them as easily as a second skin. "But I don't know the restomod business specifics."

"Exactly," Nova nearly spat.

She choked on the suggestion she knew she had to make twice before she could force it out through clenched teeth. "So what do you think about Mr. Davis and I teaming up?"

This time Eli couldn't contain his guffaw. "*Mr.* Davis. Who the hell is that?"

It surprised her more though when Kaige snarled. "Don't call me that. Reminds me of my fucking father. I'm nothing like him."

Still, he glanced at the floor, away from her for the first time, when he denied it.

"Fine. *Super Nova.*" She barely refrained from rolling her eyes. "He could help me vet my ideas before committing them to the plan and wasting time chasing dead ends."

"Can you do that?" Eli raised a brow at Nova.

"I'm not an idiot, you know." He crossed his arms in a way that highlighted the bulges of his biceps. "I'll show her my plans if it's what's best for Hot Rods."

***

"Wait. You have your new business concepts formalized somewhere? Like in a proposal or something? I thought you just had them up here." Eli tapped his temple with his index finger.

"Nope. They're on my laptop. Been honing them for a while." Kaige turned serious for a moment. When he dropped his thug routine, she had to swallow hard. Beneath his resentment, there lingered a whole lot of hurt. The flex of his throat, the shuffling of his boots and the wringing of his damaged knuckles said it all.

Nola imagined him pouring himself into the improvements he wanted to pitch to Eli. For endless hours, fiddling with them at night, after Cobra retired to the rooms he shared with Alanso and Sally.

Suddenly, she could understand maybe a tiny bit of Nova's frustration. She'd fume too if the chance to show off her work had been stolen. Even if they partnered now, the guys would think she had influenced him, generating the new goals he hoped to pursue.

For one second, she pitied him.

And then he ruined it by opening his big, dumb mouth. "As long as Hot Rods thrives, I don't give a shit who gets credit for being the brainiac behind it. I'm no glory hound, and I don't need some bullet point on a fancy resume like *Ms. Brown* here. Besides, it's what your dad would ask of me."

Eli scrubbed his hand over his face, pinching the bridge of his nose. The way the trio had spoken of Tom London during their consultation with her sister made his importance to the group clear. A low blow, bringing the man into this discussion. Or maybe genuine concern. Would Kaige put aside his differences to make the guy proud?

Nola bet the answer was yes.

Why couldn't this damn assignment have been easy? Emotional landmines scattered across their playing field.

"You're right. Dad would want us to collaborate. So why haven't I seen these roadmaps for the shop?" Scratching his head, Eli narrowed his eyes a bit.

Nola held her breath as something heavy seemed to pass between the two friends, who seemed a hell of a lot more like brothers than pals. At least they shared the same capacity for communicating a whole lot with a few words, just like she and her sister did.

"You've been busy. I didn't want to bug you. Plus there are a few kinks I was still working out." A shrug loosened some of the knots in Kaige's shoulders for the first time. "Your girl Nola here can help me brainstorm how to get around the roadblocks. I guess that would be okay."

The first sign of thawing had Nola perking up. Maybe it wasn't hopeless.

"Hey, I didn't mean to step on your toes." A wince slashed Eli's face. "I screwed this up. But in the end I think we're going to get where we need to go. I'm sorry, Kaige."

"It's okay, Eli." And it seemed as if it was. The air between the guys cleared and Nola could breathe again. Definitely similar to her and her sister. Sure, they'd fought plenty. Still, it was easy to forgive someone you loved even when they made a bonehead move. Because deep down you knew there had been no malice behind it. "*We're* okay."

Nola stared at her hands, clutched tightly in her lap. She felt as if she'd intruded on their bonding. And damn if it didn't make her like both men just a little more.

Eli stood, abandoning the red leather seat behind his desk to lay his hand on Kaige's shoulder. It surprised the hell out of her when the bitter man flashed a sense of humor.

"Now get your ass in gear. You've got guests to invite to a par-tay." Kaige grinned as he slapped the other guy on the ass. The dazzling display of his crooked grin, not to mention the blatant affection her temporary teammate demonstrated for his boss, had her drawing a sharp breath.

Ah, hell. She'd better get used to it if she planned to stick around. After all, Cobra was unconventional—in love with both a woman and man. If she was to stay, she'd have to broaden her horizons a bit.

Somehow she thought that might not be such a terrible thing.

"Is there anything else to discuss, then?" Eli leaned forward, eager to shake on their arrangement.

"One thing." She stood so they were as close to eye-level as possible. It might sound funny, but she wasn't joking around.

"Uh-oh." He grinned. "Let's hear it."

"If this dirtbag gives me any trouble, I get to kick him in the nuts." Nola jerked her head toward Kaige.

Super Nova laughed. For one glorious moment, the pure bliss transformed him into something entirely too tempting—a mechanical God who'd be sure to tune her engine just right. When he caught her wide-eyed stare, he stifled the ringing mid-chuckle as if pissed he'd gotten busted finding her amusing.

Nola couldn't help the barest of smiles she flashed in his direction.

"Deal." Eli extended his hand and she took it. "Use the rest of the day to get prepared, and we'll see you back here tomorrow."

"Will do."

It surprised her when Kaige Davis held the office door for her as she left. On impulse, she reached into her purse and snagged one of her business cards then tucked it in the breast pocket of his grease-spotted Hot Rods uniform as she squeezed past.

When he simply stared at her, she thought maybe he hadn't been attempting politeness. No, maybe he was eager to see her taillights. Oh well.

CHAPTER THREE

Nola took a deep breath when the front door opened and her sister, Amber, called out a greeting. She stretched before abandoning her laptop and the copious notes strewn across a quarter of the pages in her notebook to go on the hunt for a snack. How could it be nearly ten o'clock already?

She hardly remembered eating the grilled cheese her mom had brought her for lunch or the chef salad she'd shoveled in her mouth with one hand while researching everything from cars to mechanical equipment online. More than ever, she wanted to walk into Hot Rods prepared tomorrow.

"Hey." She smiled at her sister, who looked worn yet grinned from ear to ear. Hard work didn't scare either of them so long as they answered to themselves while helping their clients.

"How'd it go today?" Amber asked.

"Okay." She shrugged. "Mostly a meet-and-greet with the jerk Eli told us about. The real fun starts tomorrow."

"Oh jeez." Amber let her head drop back as she studied the stained-glass lamp that had come straight out of the '50s into their modest yet neat kitchen. They shared the house with their mother. Shelter ranked higher in their priorities than décor.

"What?" Nola splayed her hands in front of her. "I didn't do anything, I swear. He hated me on sight."

At the sound of the sisters chatting, their mom ventured into the kitchen in her soft pink robe and matching slippers. Though the set had a couple frayed edges, her frugal nature wouldn't allow them to replace the somewhat faded loungewear, though they could afford to these days.

Hard times had ensured they remained fiscally conservative.

Just in case.

"Why are you looking so guilty, Nola?" Her mom tipped her head as she flipped on her parental super senses and joined the fray.

"I'm not!" She might have squeaked as she reached for the utensil drawer. "Look, one of the clients seems to have a giant stick up his perfect ass. I didn't put it there. But I'm sure as hell going to have to deal with him being cranky about whoever or whatever did."

"So he's hot *and* ornery?" Amber winced. "Yikes. Never a good combo."

"It's nothing I can't handle." Nola used her hip to close the drawer and tucked the spoon in her mouth as she opened the freezer to grab the half-pint of salty caramel ice cream she'd stashed.

Who could blame a girl for a little stress eating the night before a big job began?

Her mother raised one brow. "That's the good stuff—he must be *really* sexy. Or really difficult. I don't want you alone with a crazy man if he's got some kind of turf issue."

"It's not like that, Mom." She shrugged. "I kind of think maybe Eli didn't realize that his friend had ideas of his own for the shop."

"Even worse," her mom objected. "You'll get caught in the crossfire."

"Plus, she said he's hot. Don't forget that." Amber knocked her shoulder into their mom's. "When's the last time she admitted that about any man?"

"True." Her mom sighed. "Not even that blond vampire guy on that show you like."

"Ick." Nola wrinkled her nose. "Too girly."

"And that's not a problem with your grease monkey?" Amber wriggled her brows.

"Stop. He's not mine. Except as a very unwilling business partner." She dug into the frozen treat more energetically than the poor dairy delight demanded. "Anyway, how did the wedding planning go?"

"Great." Her sister lit up as she began to tick off the monumental progress she'd made in a single twenty-four-hour period. She would work miracles for the trio they'd both been captivated by. True love was impossible to miss. Or admire.

Their mother cleared her throat.

"Yeah?" Amber paused the recounting of her conquest in scheduling the city's most up-and-coming baker to design a cake on such short notice, under budget too.

"I just thought of something."

"What, Mom?" Nola paused with her spoon midair.

"What if the guy, the one who's giving you crap... What if he's grumpy because he's resentful?" She tapped her chin thoughtfully.

"Of what?" Nola and her sister said at the same time.

"Didn't you say the guys have been part of the shop since they were teenagers? Along with that girl, Sally? What if he wanted her for himself? Or what if he wanted one of those other two guys—Eli or Alanso?" Their mom searched for the right words, trying to be politically correct, but they didn't know a lot of openly polyamorous people.

Okay, exactly three.

"You're saying you think Kaige might be in love with Sally?" Nola offered.

"Or Eli. Or Alanso. Maybe he's gay," Amber added.

"It's not like he had some kind of indicator tattoo on his forehead. Hell, it's one of the few places he doesn't have ink." Nola tried not to sigh at the memory of those bold slashes of color. "But no…I really don't think he's gay."

The way he'd checked out her breasts, and her hips, and kept touching her leg…

Intuition screamed at her that if they'd met under different circumstances, like at a bar, they'd have been in for a wild ride. First she'd have to actually go out, though. She and Amber had turned into homebodies as they'd nurtured their consulting business.

"He could be bi. Mom's right." Amber shrugged without malice. "It's a possibility. There are no rules in this kind of relationship, are there? Well, I guess there have to be, but we don't know what they are. Maybe you stepped in the middle of something a lot more sensitive than we realized."

And why did that thought make Nola turn a little green?

"Don't wrinkle your nose like that, Nola Macey Brown." Her mom wagged her finger. "There's nothing wrong with people loving each other, no matter who they are. Girls, boys, blacks, whites, whatever. Two, three, ten, it doesn't make any difference as long as they're honest and all agree."

"Of course not, Mom." Nola ducked her head, her cheeks heating as she recalled plenty of stories about her father, and how—before his death—he'd constantly been harassed by racists for his dark-skinned wife. Back then, in the deep South, things had been different.

"She's not discriminating or being snobby." Amber laughed. "She's *jealous*. He must have been one serious hottie, this mechanic."

Their mom grinned as she looked between her daughters, confirming Amber's diagnosis.

"It doesn't matter how smokin' he is." Nola turned to replace the rest of her ice cream in the freezer, her appetite vanished. "He's still an asshat."

"Is your asshat's name Kaige Davis?" Amber asked, a bit too innocently as she toyed with Nola's laptop.

"Yes. Why?" She let the refrigerator door slam closed, despite the glare from her mother, then trotted to her sister's side.

And there she saw it.

A bolded message had appeared in her inbox from Super Nova, with the subject line: *Sorry, I'm a dumbass*.

"Well, go ahead." Her mother poked her in the shoulder. "Read it."

"No way!" Nola shrieked as her sister tried to click the note. Reaching forward, she snatched the laptop off the table and dashed to her room for some privacy, shutting the door behind her.

The hollow-core didn't keep the tinkling laughter her mother and sister exchanged from creeping after her.

She smiled, though her finger trembled, as she tapped the key to see what her new partner had to say for himself.

***

Kaige flipped the business card Nola had given him over and over across his bruised knuckles. Like her, the sturdy cardstock was dark, sleek and engaging. He rubbed the pad of his thumb over her embossed email address, wishing it were her plump lips he touched instead.

61

Shit. Sometime in the past few hours, his anger had blown over. Something equally as hot, but a lot more steamy, had replaced it the more he thought about the woman who'd refused to take his shit in their meeting this morning.

It was as if he'd gone from denting his precious bumper to having the whole thing fall right off. Because working with her would be ten times harder if he was horny than if he was pissed off.

Plus, she'd earned his respect. And he didn't treat people he admired like crap.

At least he could man up and explain himself before they were official partners. It would be easier to compose his feelings and send them to her than to try and muddle through a verbal apology. He wasn't usually great at organizing his thoughts or keeping his cool long enough to express what he intended.

So he grabbed his laptop, plopped into bed and leaned against the headboard as he started a message to the sassy consultant, then deleted it. About a hundred times in a row.

Frustrated, he hammered out *Sorry, I'm a dumbass* in the subject line.

The cursor sat in the body of the email, blinking at him like a check engine light on the fritz. It refused to stop no matter how he finessed the chaos in his mind. Irritating and persistent, it distracted him from finding the right thing to say.

Eventually he came up with a single line.

I'm not perfect on my best days, but I'll try to be less of a fuck up tomorrow. Nova

A simple truth, but a motto he'd lived by ever since coming to the Hot Rods. Continuous improvement. Tom had given him that goal once, and it had stuck. He held himself to higher standards every day, even if he didn't always succeed in achieving them.

Cheers erupted from the living room as someone won a race on their latest videogame. A pause followed. It might have lasted several minutes. Then more shouts and good-natured curses. Again. Then again.

Still the cursor flashed at him.

"Ah, fuck it." Kaige clicked *Send*.

He wandered out into the main room with his computer in one arm. Along the way, he rummaged a slice of room-temperature pepperoni pizza from the jumble of boxes on the island. Then he slumped into a free space on the massive sectional couch, propping his laptop on one thigh as he demolished the second go at dinner.

He hadn't sat there very long, wishing he could recall the damn email he'd sent Nola, when a soft *ding* drew his attention away from the rematch taking place on the big-screen in front of him.

Nola was efficient and prompt in answering correspondence. Why wasn't he surprised?

What did kind of sneak up on him was the thrill that zinged along his spine at the sight of her name, while he clicked the email in his inbox and anticipated her response as it loaded in the main pane of his browser.

No one's perfect, I only ask that you're halfway civilized. ~Nola

A smirk kicked up the corners of his mouth. She hadn't rubbed his face in his apology or made him defensive with some kind of righteous attack, though she would have been justified in launching one.

That's a tall order. Did you see the guys I live with? None of us have very good manners. Kaige

P.S. Didn't you mean ~Ms. Brown?

He failed to mention how he'd wiped pizza grease on his sweats to answer her right away.

I can teach you.

Rule one, don't growl at people you've just met.

Rule two, don't stare at my boobs.

~Nola

Kaige laughed out loud, drawing curious stares from Bryce and Holden, who were sitting this race out. "Uh, some dumb video on YouTube."

"Show me." Carver scooted closer. "I've had about as much of Alanso kicking everyone's ass as usual as I can stand. Why is that fucker so damn good at videogames?"

Kaige ignored his friend's rhetorical question and the middle finger Al shot in their direction without pausing his winning streak.

"I closed it already." Nova angled the screen away from Meep when another message followed hot on the heels of the one he hadn't even replied to yet.

I almost forgot...

Rule three, don't question your boss's intentions. He was too sexed up to realize he hurt your feelings by not soliciting your ideas.

~Nola

Nova took her insightful response like a fist to the gut. He sucked in a breath then looked around to see if anyone had noticed. Barracuda glanced over, then went back to reading a transmission manual while Holden surfed the net on his tablet, probably looking for new salvage lots they could raid.

Kaige cleared his throat and tried to ignore the tremble in his hands when he pecked at the keyboard. The stiffness there had nothing to do with his banged-up knuckles. They were healing nice and quick.

Shit, I was that obvious? It's my fault too. I didn't show him my plans. But yeah, it pissed me off when I assumed he thought I was too dumb to handle the future of the shop without giving me a real shot first. That had nothing to do with you. I really am sorry. I shouldn't have taken it out on you.

NoVa

P.S. I like that our names kind of match.

This time the words came easily. With her helping him find a constructive outlet, he could communicate the thoughts that had been jammed in his mind for hours. If she could do the same at translating his strategies from concept to concrete expressions, they might have a chance at making this thing work after all.

Apology accepted.

Ha ha, I guess they do. I probably would have noticed sooner if my eyes weren't starting to cross. I've been looking at the computer too long!

~NoLa

He glanced at the clock above the TV. It was after midnight already, crap.

I didn't realize it was so late. Am I keeping you up?

Nova

Though he'd had the early shift most mornings lately, he hadn't once yawned or felt the need to rub his eyes tonight. This could be a really bad sign. If it wasn't way past their babies' bedtimes, he would have Facetimed one of Joe's Powertools crew for some advice he didn't feel like asking his Hot Rods about just yet.

That might have been a first. Another *ding* caught his attention.

Nope. I've been doing my homework. I have a lot of questions for you.

~Nola

Kaige's heart *kathumped* like a car with a catastrophic flat. Was she talking about his history? Had she looked up the youth center where Tom had found him? A few news articles and PR pieces from the past decade might be lingering out in cyberspace somewhere. Would she ask about stuff he didn't plan to unearth?

As if she could read his unease in his lack of snappy response, she sent a double message.

About the market, I mean. I know a ton about business. Not so much about cars.

Will you be my tutor? ☺

~Nola

The only other people he'd ever met who grasped when to pry and when to back off so seamlessly were the Hot Rods, because they had shady pasts too. He considered her street-tough attitude earlier as well. Could Nola have some dark spots of her own? Could she understand?

Getting ahead of yourself there, Nova, he chastised himself.

Don't make me picture you wearing a plaid skirt and knee-high socks. Besides, you must know some stuff. You own a car, don't you? What kind? Nova

He opted for humor instead of the more serious path this conversation could have veered down if he let it.

As he hoped, he unleashed her tiger. Too bad he couldn't see it, though he could picture it after her brief displays earlier.

Rule two, Nova. Remember, rule two.

A crappy red one. No seriously, I'd have to go look. It's just a way to get from here to there. Most of the time it doesn't even break down.

~Nola

Kaige grinned, then typed. *I didn't say a word about your rack.*

And you're killing me here.

Nova

He clicked the refresh button on his inbox about thirty times in ten seconds.

Careful or I'll beat your fine ass with a ruler. I meant what I said to Eli. About the nut kicking.

Don't worry about my car. It's had a good life. ~Nola

He snorted, then tried to fake a sneeze when Sally peeked over at him, her eyes wide and unblinking. *You think I have a nice ass? Nova*

Okay, that's it. I'm done here. I have a hell of a lot more research to do if I'm going to impress you tomorrow. ~Nola

You've already done that. A bunch. Nova

This time her reply was simple. And he could read the seriousness in the two words. Maybe she even referred to more than his compliment. He hoped she meant them for reaching out after he'd nearly wrecked everything. *Thank you. ~Nola*

It was weird how most times in email, meanings could be lost, but when he talked to Nola, everything seemed clear.

You're welcome. Seriously. My garage is your garage. Don't work too hard, though. I'm looking forward to seeing you bright and early tomorrow. Nova

Same goes, Kaige. Good night. ~N

Good night, Nola. The other N

Kaige waited fifteen minutes. Long enough to be sure she'd taken his advice and gone to bed. Thoughts of her long legs sliding beneath her sheets had him clearing his throat and making a break for his room.

He held his computer in front of his crotch like a shield, hoping he could make it to jerk off before anyone stopped him. While they might find another way to relieve him, it didn't feel right to fantasize about Nola while someone else touched him.

So he dashed to his room, slamming the door harder than intended, and took matters into his own hands.

***

Nola had barely removed her key from the ignition when Kaige crossed the lot in her direction.

She smiled when he opened her door and gave her a hand out. "Good morning, Super Nova."

"You were pretty much right about your car." He tempered the insult with a grin.

"Hey." Nola whacked him in what had to be a six-pack with the back of her hand before she thought better of it. Her fingers bounced right off. "It gets the job done."

"That's like the difference between a cheap vibrator and good sex." He grinned as they picked up right where they'd left off the night before.

"It gets the job done," she repeated with a shrug and strutted off before he could add anything spicier than she could stomach, though she wondered what his car looked like and how well he drove it.

Somehow she didn't doubt either his machine or his handling were less than spectacular.

While she felt like she'd won him over—Eli, Alanso and Sally too—she still hadn't met half the gang. First impressions mattered. She didn't want them to think she mixed business with pleasure to get her way.

Despite the height of her heels, she strode to the garage's office and let herself inside as Kaige jogged to catch up from where she'd left him, staring with his jaw open, in her dust.

"Glad to see you back." Eli acknowledged her entrance with a nod.

Had he been waiting for her to run? To call and say she'd reconsidered?

"You're not going to shake me that easily," she promised.

"Great." He smiled, then addressed the man coming up behind her. "Alanso and I set up a whiteboard and some supplies along with your laptop in the break room, Super Nova."

"Time to get to work then." Kaige closed his hand around hers, leading her toward the garage and their new pseudo space. His touch warmed her right down to her toes, which curled.

"Well, I thought I'd introduce Ms. Brown to the gang first." Eli eyed Nova warily, as if waiting for him to spring some kind of trap.

Nola suspected he had another prize in mind after their conversation last night.

"I'll show her around, Cobra. If the goal is for you to concentrate on pulling together the wedding, then you'd better quit screwing around with us. Two weeks sounds friggin' impossible, but what do I know? I've never even been to a wedding before." He shrugged.

"Really? Never?" Nola faced him, her head tilted a little. Genuine curiosity drew her to the desolation she caught flickering through his gaze from time to time. She was glad he'd have this experience to share with his friends. Unless her mom and sister had been right.

What if he was jealous?

"Are you sure?" Eli asked at the same time Nola spoke. He had to be wondering if Kaige's about-face was genuine. It was as drastic as punk kids doing donuts in the middle of an abandoned parking lot before delivering meals to elderly people in their neighborhood. "Ms. Brown's sister—"

"Really, Eli." She reminded him again, "Call me Nola. My sister is Amber. Otherwise, I'll start referring to you as Mr. London."

Both Eli and Kaige laughed at that.

"What?" She tried not to catch their infectious smiles.

"You'll meet Tom soon." Kaige squeezed her hand, reminding her that he hadn't let go. "Eli's father. He's…"

"All of the Hot Rods' dad." Cobra finished when Nova stumbled. "Anyway, yeah… Amber worked some miracles and got us everything we needed. The catch is the officiator. She's booked every other weekend this summer. Our only shot is the Saturday after next. Otherwise, we have to wait until fall. Frankly, the sooner the better, in my book. I've been tasked with calling people to invite them personally since we don't have enough time— or really any desire—to do the whole fancy mailing, calligraphy bullshit."

"Sounds like you'd better get your ass in gear." Nova used his free hand to smack Eli's aforementioned buns, then continued tugging her toward their main workspace.

Nola tried desperately not to gawk as the bond between the Hot Rods became more and more evident. She'd never seen men work so intimately as a team. Their friendship—and even that seemed like a weak label for what she witnessed—glowed bright and strong.

Making mental notes, she put a giant checkmark next to charisma as one of the garage's strengths. Customers would be able to sense the energy they kept around them and the love they had for their labors. Essence like that couldn't be taught and it had no price tag when it came to giving a business that extra, indefinable *something* that would bring clients flocking in and staying loyal. A huge point in their favor already.

Though Kaige had come on strong, making no excuses for his familiarity after last night's email exchange, she couldn't muster up the willpower to shake loose from his grip. She pretended she worried about her stilettos slipping on the painted concrete floor instead of admitting the man had some kind of spell on her. Nova tempted her to ditch what she thought of as her professional costume and be herself. The *real* Nola Brown. Something she refused to do at work ordinarily. Confusing her career with her personal life had never been an issue.

She didn't plan for that poor judgment to begin today either.

First up, Kaige led her to the gap between two cars. Both were lifted to waist level. Delicious, very able-bodied men lounged partially beneath them. Dirt and grease only added to their lethal sex appeal.

"Barracuda, Meep, roll out for a minute." Kaige knocked the steel-toe of his scuffed black boot against a wooden dolly. "There's somebody here I'd like you to meet."

Warmth radiated from Kaige's broad hand as he finally relinquished hers. Instead of using it to cradle her fingers, he settled it in the dip of her waist and guided her nearer to his hard body to avoid any accidental contact from his fellow garagemates. Nola had to restrain herself. Otherwise she would be purring like a kitten and curling closer to his protective touch.

This was bad.

Really bad.

From their website profiles, she knew the pair as Roman and Carver, though she tacked their nicknames on to the mental outline she assembled for each man.

As the guys unfurled themselves and stood, the *whrrrp* of a pneumatic impact wrench—at least she guessed that's what the tool was from her studies the night before—grew silent. The racket echoed then faded, sounding less like pit road at one of the stock car races her sister liked to scout for hot racers and more like an empty hall.

Amber would die when she heard today's updates on Nola's new assignment.

Her sister could keep stinky wedding duty.

Kaige called over his shoulder, "Hey, Bryce. Grab Swinger and come here a minute, would you?"

Nola couldn't quite make out the grumbled response, in a bass so deep it defied her hearing, but Carver must have been better at deciphering his friend's speech. He translated for her. "He's coming, just needed to finish screwing something in."

"If you weren't here, we'd probably make a crass joke about Rebel's ability to screw." Kaige winked at her, still with that damn hand on her. When she tried to step away, he shifted to maintain contact. Heat seeped through her blazer and the thin silk blouse beneath it straight into her spine, making it as limber and melty as the rest of her insides.

Another pair of mechanics joined their semicircle when beckoned, completely overloading her with their potent testosterone barrage. Roman and Carver were wirier compared to the bulk of Bryce or the sleek yet defined muscles Holden sported.

Each of them took turns giving her a wave instead of a handshake since they claimed they didn't want to muss her up. She wondered for a moment if they were sensing some of the stake Kaige had made.

Half of her didn't mind in the least, the other portion was outraged. Determining the appropriate response was impossible when caught in the crosshairs of their intense scrutiny. Their deceptively relaxed postures, leaning against toolboxes or a stack of wheels, didn't fool her in the least. They sized her up like a pack of dogs circling prey or maybe a potential mate.

"Nola and Nova." Holden chuckled. "You sorta rhyme. How cute!"

Kaige glowered at his friend—Swinger, they'd called him. How would she ever learn their names *and* their nicknames?

Nova's sour face only proved he was hot no matter what. Damn, when had she ever seen a man as fine as him?

Not even on TV.

His Ken-doll coloration could have made him too pretty if it weren't for all the other pure maleness on top. Scruff roughed up his jaw, shadowing his paler skin with stubble. His dreads were messy chic, and impressive for a white boy. Bold, colorful tattoos drew her attention to his sculpted arms. They peeked out from beneath the grease-stained white wife-beater that he wore beneath navy-blue coveralls embroidered with the Hot Rods logo, now bunched around his waist.

Some evil part of her yearned to tug, just a little, and bare his high, tight ass. Though she'd refused to answer him in their emails. *Hell, yeah.* She had nothing to complain about there.

Nola shifted her weight from one high heel to the other, pressing her thighs together as subtly as possible. She played with the buttons on her blouse while she waited for someone to break their awkward silence.

"Just so you know, you don't have to dress like a stuffy old librarian to be taken seriously around here." Bryce's wide smile took the edge of his bluntness. "Jeans and a T-shirt would be more practical. Feel free to go slobby, like us."

"Don't mind him." Holden smacked the big guy in the gut. His fist bounced off as though it were a gnat. "Rebel hates formalities of any type."

"I like to think I measure a person's worth on their actions, not their presentation of themselves to the world or by any physical belongings they possess." Bryce's quiet, persuasive tone demonstrated why he held the customer service position in the group. Reserved, yet eloquent, he navigated tricky waters with ease.

It was apparent that money meant nothing to him as a gauge for wealth. Nola could understand. She'd done her research last night and found they'd all been taken in by Tom London. Like her and Amber, none of them had started the game of life with an unfair advantage handed down by their parents.

They hadn't had shit to their names. It hadn't changed who they were. Not Nola, or her sister. And it didn't seem like it had impacted these guys either. The most valuable things they had came from within. Honor and dignity measured above everything.

She could relate.

A tendril of admiration wove through her, only increasing her damned attraction to the man beside her and his pretty awesome friends. *Keep your mind on business. Helping out their garage will be the best you can do for all of you.*

"Then again..." Bryce's smile spread as he scanned her from head to toe. "Kaige has a thing for women in heels. You know, if you want to butter him up."

Nola sputtered a bit at the revelation. It should have been an innocent remark. The last thing she wanted was for them to think she was coming on to them, Kaige especially. When the rest of the men laughed, she gave in to the sense of humor she could sense twinkling in their eyes.

Maybe they were right. This professional ruse didn't suit her. Most times she needed it to get her employers to take her seriously. Young and attractive didn't always make for a good combination in her role.

Unable to help herself, she relaxed a bit. A giggle escaped her despite her belated attempt to clench her teeth. "Okay, I'll see if I can do better tomorrow."

With that, the crowd dispersed. The guys got back to work. Serious about their jobs, and loving what they did, they didn't waste precious Hot Rods time though their shouted jeers and the music pumping from the radio they turned up chased after her and Kaige as they rounded a corner at the back of the garage.

She checked out their state-of-the-art equipment—impressed as she mentally compared it to the stuff she'd dug up on the Internet—and the neat, orderly shop layout. They may have been involved in dirty work, but they kept their areas tidy. This was no fly-by-night operation. From her brief analysis, she could tell the business was healthy.

A wave of disappointment snaked through her guts. They may not need the services of Brown & Brown after all. If her assessment today, after peeking at Kaige's plans, left her with that impression, she'd say so. Scamming customers wasn't a cornerstone of her own model.

From the quality of the workmanship around her, ripping people off wasn't a tenant of the Hot Rods trade either. The more she learned about them, the more esteem she had for the seven guys and one woman who'd built this domain from the ground up.

Her heels tapped on the sealed concrete.

Kaige never took his cupped hand from her elbow. His thumb brushed an arc over the sensitive skin there. "Careful now, it's slippery sometimes. Mustang Sally does her painting and polishing back here. We've busted our asses a few times when wax spills on the floor. It's funny to see Carver or Alanso doing their banana-peel routine. Wouldn't want you to hurt yourself, though."

The genuine affection in his tone turned her on even more. Thank God she *had* worn her thick jacket, despite the searing temperatures outside. Otherwise it'd probably be very apparent that her nipples were about to jab through her lace bra.

Kaige poked his head around the corner, into an open doorway. "Sally? You there, Mustang?"

"Come in. I haven't started taping the Schultz job yet." The crisp answer seemed at odds with the tough young woman Nola spotted covered in paint-splattered coveralls that matched the rest of the gang's. Her jet-black hair was pulled back today and covered with a Louis Vuitton handkerchief. She stood up straight, though that didn't make her very tall, especially not with Kaige and two other men nearby.

The woman had immediately earned the envy of Nola and her sister when she'd showed up to her wedding planning appointment sandwiched between two drop-dead gorgeous men and announced she needed help in staging a non-traditional commitment ceremony. To bind her to both of them.

Alanso, the bald Latino guy Nola had also met briefly then, hovered by Sally's side. An older man, who looked far too much like Eli to be anyone other than his father, half-sat on a drawing table in the corner.

Damn, even with a few decades on him, the guy had sex appeal in spades.

"Good morning, you lucky bitch you." Nola didn't hesitate. She took Bryce's helpful hint about casual, genuine interactions to heart. Trusting her intuition, she stepped forward and hugged Sally.

"Hey, plenty more Hot Rods where mine came from. Feel free to take a pair home with you. Less hassle around here."

Mustang may have teased, but her shrewd gaze flicked between Nola and Kaige. She smiled as she nuzzled into Alanso's chest. "You remember my future husband."

"Of course, how could I forget a handsome devil like him?" Nola nodded as he murmured something in Spanish. She didn't understand his words, but the tone was enough to leave her gooey inside. "And you must be Tom London."

Nola didn't wait to be introduced. Instead, she stuck out her hand.

"I'm so pleased to meet you." His mouth curved up slightly as he measured her. It'd been a long time since Nola had craved someone's approval as badly as this man's. From everything she'd read about him last night, he deserved every bit of the reverence and respect she saw in Kaige's eyes when he looked at the guy who'd become his de facto father.

It was no surprise to find Mr. London lounging around the shop, since he'd opened the pumping station himself when he was younger than his sons were now. Today's visit couldn't be an accident, though, not right when she had been expected.

The guy kept a close eye on his extended family. But why would he consider her a threat?

She was sure he did when it took a full fifteen seconds at least—which felt like an eternity under his intense stare—for his smile to turn sincere and his eyes to warm. After peeking up toward Kaige and finding the guy grinning right back, Tom used the grip he still had on her hand to tug her inward and give her a hug.

"Thanks for keeping these kids in line." He patted her back.

"I'm glad to be working with the Hot Rods." She didn't have to fake her enthusiasm as she did sometimes with the corporations she optimized. At least here a large part of the profits went to fund charitable work at the community center. A cause she could wholeheartedly support. "And honestly, it's an honor. I appreciate your work with the London Center. You're truly an inspiration."

"Well, look at that." Kaige slapped his surrogate dad on the back. "I haven't seen you blush in…ever, actually."

"Shut it, kid." Tom mock-glared then added, "And don't forget the ten bucks you owe me for losing our bet."

Alanso laughed, his arm still slung around Sally as Nova paid up for something she was sure she didn't want to know about. What a family. It made Nola's heart ache to see the support system they'd constructed. Sure, she had Amber, but sometimes it felt like it was the two of them against the world since their mom hadn't always been in fighting form.

Not that they'd crumble beneath those odds.

"Aw, Tom, you're so sweet." Sally added fuel to the fire.

"I'm sorry. I didn't mean to embarrass you. It's just that my sister and I had to use the services at the center ourselves. Awhile ago. Obviously. I'll never forget how grateful we were for a few hot meals and a place to take a shower that winter we lived in our mother's car." Nola cleared her throat. She tried to keep her fingers still against her skirt as she joked, "It's hell washing your hair in a mall sink all the time. Worse when you only get half-finished because the security guards catch on and chase you away before you can rinse out the shampoo. Running with that junk in your eyes isn't pretty. The center staff always had open arms."

Kaige must have noticed her discomfort. He immediately claimed one of her hands and knitted his fingers with hers. He squeezed gently, starting up with that maddening rub of his thumb again. Only this time it soothed her as she hoped he'd intended.

"The gift of my wife's work keeps improving people's lives, even though it's been so long since she left us." Tom's expression nearly broke Nola's heart. Mrs. London had to have died fifteen years ago by now, and yet he spoke of her with such love, Nola knew he'd never moved on. Probably never would. She understood that too. Watching her mother grieve had been a hell of a lot harder than calling their beat-up Explorer home. "I'm glad we were able to help, even a little bit, in tiding you over until you could get on your feet. You should be proud. My son tells me you and your sister have built quite a strong enterprise for yourselves too. He's no dummy. He wouldn't trust your family with the most important day of his life if you didn't deserve his faith. And he certainly wouldn't have invited you here, to meddle with his baby. You're doing a great job, Nola."

And with his paternal praise, Tom made her feel like part of his clan.

When had anyone encouraged her before? Though her mom probably would have if not buried in grief, she hadn't always been in a position to offer support.

Tears stung Nola's eyes. She blinked rapidly, not wanting to appear weak during her first real day on the job. How could somewhere instantly feel like home? And what would happen when her temporary assignment ended?

This wasn't her place. These weren't her insta-friends. Even if they seemed like it.

All she could do was live up to the compliment Tom had paid her. "So I guess we should get started then?"

She didn't realize she nibbled her lower lip until Kaige lifted his free hand to swipe his thumb over the abused flesh. "I'm ready if you are."

Something flashed in his sky-blue gaze. Empathy maybe. Not pity. She'd come to know what that looked like well enough during those tough times. A guy who could understand where she'd been and that it didn't make her any less capable, well that was something she'd struggled to find.

And here he was, holding her hand.

"Have fun, kids." Tom broke them from their daze. "Don't work too hard."

"Don't listen to him, *cabron*." Alanso got his say in. "Make us rich."

Sally laughed and slapped him playfully. His tight abs sounded like a drumhead when she tapped him. "Quit being ridiculous."

"Hey, we're gonna need the cash once Eli sees the bill for that gown you and Nola's sister picked out last night." He pretended to gripe, "Since when do you even like dresses?"

"If I'm only going to wear one once, it'd better be the perfect getup." Sally shrugged, looking sheepish.

"You'll be beautiful as always, I'm sure." Alanso tipped her face up and kissed her softly.

Nola had to look away. Not because she felt like she was intruding, but because she wrestled envy at the tenderness and adoration Alanso rained on his soon-to-be wife.

"Although I like you just fine in nothing too." He broke the spell, returning their easy camaraderie.

"All right, enough clowning around." Kaige nudged her out the door. "We'll be in the break room if you need us. Don't need us."

Something in his warning made it sound as if they'd be getting busy. And not the kind of involved that had to do with marketing strategies or new product development either.

Part of her didn't object as strenuously as it should.

"But my leftover pizza is in the fridge." Alanso pouted. "I'll give you until lunchtime. Then I'm coming in."

"Fair enough." Kaige wiggled his brows. "We can get a lot accomplished in a few hours. Right, babe?"

The thrill of his pet name shouldn't have affected her. But it did.

Everything about him did.

Crap.

Nola wouldn't do anything to jeopardize Tom's opinion of her, and even more importantly, of her sister or their business. Certainly not by fooling around with one of the Hot Rods while on the clock.

Yet once they were sequestered in the break room, with its big folding table in the center and a whiteboard propped against one wall, she realized Kaige didn't intend to drop the ball either. Though he pulled his chair unnecessarily close to hers while firing up his laptop and he occasionally touched her knee—or caressed her hand or brushed a stray hair from her cheek—while they poured over his financial documents, he kept generally focused on the meat of the matter.

The success of Hot Rods.

By the time he'd moved from theoretical explanations of future product lines and services he'd like to expand then walked her through his detailed marketing plan, she couldn't help but be impressed. The simultaneous thoroughness and boldness of his ideas turned her on even more than the ripple of his shoulder muscles as he drew a diagram on the whiteboard.

He spoke her language. And she lapped up his enthusiasm and entrepreneurial spirit.

When Alanso claimed his leftovers, she couldn't believe how the hours had flown by. And when Eli stopped in to tell them it was quitting time, she had to check her watch twice to make sure he wasn't fooling them for some unknown reason.

It seemed practical jokes were a bit of a thing between the mechanics, according to Kaige's random stories or interjections while they put their heads together and talked through the finer points of his course for the shop.

Nola collected her jacket, which she'd shed sometime after one of their laughing fits had warmed her beyond comfort. At least she told herself that's what had the temperature in the room spiking.

"So we'll see you again when?" Eli shifted his gaze between her and Kaige. He took in the scribble-covered board, seeming awed with their progress. "Tomorrow? Or do you have other clients?"

The expectant look on Kaige's face had her swallowing her instinctive denial. She'd almost told him she wouldn't be coming back. But maybe she should check out her assumptions first. "Could I have a minute to talk to Kaige before we decide?"

Eli's brows rose, but he nodded slowly. "Of course. Actually, you don't have to tell me what you work out between yourselves. I trust Kaige with anything to do with the shop. Hell, with my life. Whatever you two come up with is cool. Thanks so much for your input today. I can already tell it was worth it."

"It was a good call, Cobra." Kaige ate some crow, judging from his scowl and the way he'd charged into Eli's office yesterday morning. "Thanks."

"Anytime." Eli winked. "Make the most of the opportunity, Super Nova."

"You know I will." Kaige tossed him a mock salute. "Now get back to weddingland so I can put together a schedule with Nola."

Cobra whistled as he vanished. The cheery tune seemed to fade in the direction of Sally's studio.

CHAPTER FOUR

"So what did you want to say to me that you couldn't spill in front of Cobra?" Kaige turned toward Nola, sitting on his hand to keep it from wandering down her arm or maybe to the cleavage she'd been innocently flashing him hints of in the V of her conservative blue blouse.

How he'd like to rip that thing open, pop a button or two at least...

Once she'd finally shrugged out of her jacket, he'd been able to distinguish the finer details of her shape, which was every bit as sultry as he'd imagined. The faint shadow of what looked like a lacey bra had his imagination running wild too.

"You don't actually need my help, do you?" Nola peered up at Kaige from beneath those thick, curled lashes he'd admired all afternoon.

Working with her had been surprisingly easy. And rewarding. Finally, someone who understood his concepts and got fired up about the possibilities they represented. She'd made several great recommendations to strengthen his positions too. Her visionary way of thinking had a lot in common with his mentality, which the other guys sometimes considered a chore, eager to get in and use elbow grease to solve their problems.

So his heart dropped when she said, "I should tell your boss that my initial assessment shows it'd be unwise for him to invest in my services. All he has to do is listen to *you*. Your ideas are great. Your plan is sound. You just need to execute it now. And you don't require me for that."

It was on the tip of his tongue to speak the truth. To tell her he had it covered. But better sense refused to allow him to send her away. Everything in him screamed to pull her closer, not push her off.

"A second set of eyes is always good." He smiled. "It's cool to have someone to talk this stuff over with. It's been on my mind a lot lately, but most of the other guys aren't into pie-in-the-sky crap. And Eli's been...preoccupied."

"I bet." She chuckled, a rough yet lyrical sound that had him half-hard in an instant. He'd like to believe it was the lingering effects of the Hot Rod's recent experimentation affecting him, but he knew as much as those memories riled him, something about Ms. Nola Brown ticked all his boxes. "All right, then. I'd be glad to help. But I will include my assessment in the email summary Eli requested. It wouldn't be right for me to act like I'm more than an assistant here."

Kaige's chest puffed up, despite his best attempts to let her authentic admiration roll off his back. It felt too fucking amazing to think he might have gotten something right for once. "I think we've done enough damage in this piece-of-shit office for one day. How about we go for a ride and I'll show you some of the prototypes I laid out in these documents?"

Mostly he wanted to feel the wind in his hair and share a ride with a pretty lady.

Two of his favorite things in the world.

"Um..." She glanced at the clock then to the heap of notes she'd taken during their session. Sure, if she left now she could write up her report and have it to Eli before the end of the day, but he didn't think she was averse to long hours. Neither were the Hot Rods.

So what was holding her back?

Maybe she too felt the electricity zipping between them. Otherwise, she wouldn't hesitate to occupy the same space a little longer, he guessed.

"Chicken, Nola?" He couldn't help but goad her.

She'd flashed her cutthroat streak several times today when facilitating a way for them to crush the competition. Not through sneaky tactics. Simply by being superior to other outfits in the area. With integrity and hard work, she'd make them winners.

He liked that side of her a hell of a lot.

"Of course not. I assume you actually know how to drive these monsters you make." She sniffed and stood. "Why don't you start by showing it to me?"

He took the somewhat-valid excuse of the occasionally slick floor to rest his hand on her lower back. She fit really well in his hold. Nice enough that he imagined what it would be like to wrap his hands around her waist as he sank into her from behind. Her ass would be on prominent display, cushioning him as he plunged into her as deep as possible.

Broken from his daydream when they reached his car, he shook his head, liking the weight of his dreads as they tumbled around his face. Nola didn't mind his unusual hairstyle either if her fascinated stare was any indication.

She blinked a few times then turned her attention to his ride, as if that were any less mesmerizing. At least to him. He could stare at Nola's reflection in the flawless finish all day long. Green tint or not, she was gorgeous.

"So why this car for you?" Nola skimmed her fingers along the curve of the side mirror, one of his favorite features in the sculpture of his automobile. He appreciated the reverence in her light touch. If anyone else had marred the perfect shine, he might have gotten pissy.

Watching her admire his ride somehow felt nice.

Like she approved of his selection. Almost as if she touched part of him.

"I got kind of lucky, actually." He leaned a hip against the front quarter panel, prepared to describe his find of the century. Until something wicked dared him to take a chance. "I'll tell you the story if you go for that ride with me."

"Huh? Now?" She looked around the garage, toward the impromptu conference room as if there might be a secret exit she could dart through. "Maybe I should wait until off-hours."

"It's already after five."

"Well, until I finish my write up, I mean. Maybe another time?"

Oh no, she wouldn't dodge him.

"Your whiteboard will still be there when we get back. Hell, I'll take pictures for us and email them to you so we can do our homework tonight. I'm not talking a cross-country tour here. Enough for you to see our stuff in action. Let me show her off a bit, would you?" He edged nearer to Nola, though not close enough to invade her privacy or encourage her to bolt.

Maybe she was calculating the lesser of two evils, shunning his invite or caving to a quick spin around the block. In the end, her beautiful smile tipped up one corner of her mouth. The urge to kiss it struck Kaige hard and low in the gut.

"I don't suppose you'll let me drive?" She feigned innocence, though he wasn't fooled for an instant.

"Nope." He shrugged. It was a deal breaker. No one touched his baby except him.

"Fine." She twirled out of his reach before he could do something dumb like drag his thumb along her prominent cheekbone or taste those plump, glossy lips. "Let's hit the road."

Kaige didn't realize he grinned like a fool until he slipped on his sunglasses and caught Holden staring at them. Behind the cover of his tool chest, he flashed Kaige a thumbs up.

Damn, he didn't need the guys speculating. Plus, things were complicated these days. If he pursued a woman, he'd owe it to her to disclose his relationship with the

Hot Rods, but what a hell of a way to start down an already tricky path. Option two, he could stop playing with the guys when they got together at night.

Would that hurt them? That was the last thing Kaige wanted to do.

Maybe watching wouldn't count as cheating?

Things to think about later.

For now, he'd enjoy one of life's simplest, yet deepest, pleasures—a joy ride.

"We'll be back in a few," he called to Holden, who nodded.

A verbal response would have been lost in the din caused by his V8 engine, which roared to life right before they crawled from the garage then peeled out in the driveway.

Tom might give him hell for the maneuver later, but it'd be worth it.

Nola checked her seat belt then clapped. When she lost some of that all-business-no-play veneer, she looked ten years younger. A hundred times hotter too. Kaige peeked at the sleek length of her legs where her pencil skirt rode up. And those black heels just about killed him, especially combined with the seamed stockings she wore.

For once he was glad she thought it necessary to dress up.

"Okay, so I'm here. We're cruising..." She glanced over at him. Tendrils of hair slipped from her up-do as wind whipped through the open window. He adored that she wasn't afraid of getting disheveled. "So spill. Why this car? How'd you get lucky in it?"

Kaige wiggled his brows and confessed, "I've never scored *in* her. Not yet, anyway. Want to break that streak? I know a really pretty spot. Secluded too."

She reached over and slapped his thigh. His cock wasn't picky. It approved of the contact between his body and her long, slender fingers.

"No!" She crossed her arms, which only emphasized her perfect tits and the cleavage between them. He might have told her so if it weren't for Rule Two. "That's not what I meant. You know it. I meant, how did you pick this car for your own personal hot rod? I can see how much attention you've paid to the details. A lot of hard work and love has gone into this vehicle."

Again with the stroking! She ran one finger along the door. Her nail delicately traced the handle then the stitching in the leather. Exactly like he had minutes before he'd met her.

"Uh, right." He cleared his throat and tried to concentrate.

"Did you steal it or something?" She tipped her head, trying to interpret his hesitation.

Little did she know his stall had nothing to do with his ride and everything to do with her.

Shit, this was not how he'd planned today. Or any day, with Ms. Nola Brown.

Then again, some of life's best bits started out as surprises. Like this car.

"No. You really think I'd do something like that?" He ran one hand through his dreads before planting it on the steering wheel again then increasing their pace. Matching the curves in the road, hugging the dips and bends, he got hold of his focus. Driving always brought him clarity.

"Sorry, it was a joke." Nola reached out. She stopped short of touching him this time. It didn't matter, he could feel the heat of her hand from several inches away, or at least he imagined he could.

He nodded then moved on. "Actually, it was *almost* criminal. This car had been in a barn of a stay-at-home wife for years and years. It was pristine. Original parts, low mileage, everything a collector hopes for."

Nola hummed. "I can tell. It's so beautiful."

"Thanks, but actually, it didn't come to me perfect. I couldn't have afforded a car like this one. Immaculate. Nah, not back then. I didn't have an end-buyer's kind of cash." He didn't bother to mention that these days were different. She'd looked at the garage's profitability with him. She knew how well they did now. Pride curled his smile.

"So how *did* you get it?" She took her gaze from the landscape zipping by as they passed out of Middletown's limits and into the countryside. The pretty brown of her eyes tempted him to avert his stare from the road longer than was wise.

"Well, the woman who'd taken such good care of my baby gave it to her young college kid." He shook his head.

"Oh no! He crashed it? Was he okay?" She looked around as if she'd spot bloodstains on the carpet.

"Well, not quite the way you're thinking." Kaige chuckled as they flew over long straight roads that led to the fields surrounding their town. Onions flourished in the sun with their tall green stalks reaching toward the sunshine. Shanties and rows of workers tending the crops flashed as they passed by. He thought for a second about the mastodon skeletons they sometimes hauled from the fertile dirt that had once been the bottom of a prehistoric lake. That depression in the earth had doomed this car just as surely. "Do you remember those bad storms about eight years ago? All the farms down here flooded pretty bad."

Nola angled toward him and nodded. She tucked her knee up onto the seat, giving him one hell of a tempting shadow to try to peer into between her legs, hoping for a glimpse of pretty pink panties. No use with his sunglasses on.

"Well, this kid was coming home from college during the rain. Instead of staying on the highway, he got off and tried to use the back roads to beat the worst of the storm. But he didn't think about how rainwater pours downhill from town to here. And when he came to a part of the road..." Kaige pulled off onto the shoulder of Pumpkin Swamp Road.

"Why are we stopping?" She looked around then smacked her forehead with the palm of her hand. "Here? He tried to drive across flood water?"

"Sure did." Kaige chuckled. "I've never been to school, except what Tom made me finish. But I'm not dumb enough to try a stunt like that. It didn't take long before the car got swept away, in slow motion. Fortunately the kid, his name is Kris, was able to get out and even managed to grab his computer from the trunk. In those days it was a big clunky tower that he had to carry all the way back to Maple Avenue on the other side of the fields."

Nola's jaw hung open. "He must be strong."

"He is. And book smart. As for common sense... Well, I won't say he's stupid, but it's not a highlight." Kaige grinned. "Worst part was, he tried to push the Nova the rest of the way across. Instead it got caught in the current, arced off the road and sank into that irrigation ditch right over there."

Nola boosted herself on strong yet svelte arms. She peered toward the trench. "I can't even see the bottom. These aren't your usual side-of-the-road dips."

"Nah, this one is about eight feet deep. The car dropped like a rock. Right to the bed. And before the water receded enough for them to haul it out of here, it froze." Kaige winced when he remembered the first time he'd seen the beast. "I came out here with him and we stood on the ice, staring down at this poor baby locked in deep freeze for the winter. He sold it to me for the cost of towing."

"Sounds like he might have gotten the better end of that deal." Nola peered around her. "I would never have guessed in a million years this car had been underwater."

"Yeah. Honestly, we redid every single thing in it." Kaige ran his hands over the dash. "It took for-fucking-ever. The guys used to joke that I'd never have my own wheels. But everything inside was gutted, the frame itself had to be derusted. Then we had to treat it to keep it from degrading more. It's built from the ground up. New and classic at the same time."

"It's beautiful." As Nola scanned the car around her, he thought he detected a new appreciation in her stare. It was the hottest thing he'd ever seen. "You guys are very talented. It's no surprise Hot Rods is the best venture in Middletown these days."

"Thank you." He didn't question his instincts. Instead he unbuckled and scooted toward the center of the bench seat. Easily boxing her within reach, he lifted his hand to cup her cheek and turn her face toward him. Up close, her eyes were even warmer. Like cinnamon flakes swimming in golden apple cider on a brisk autumn day.

Her skin, which reminded him of the rich earth surrounding them, was soft beneath his calloused fingers and she smelled like peaches.

He couldn't resist temptation a second longer.

Kaige descended, pressing his parted lips to her firmly puckered frown. Undeterred, he cajoled with tiny brushes of his mouth against hers. Before long, some of the rigidity left her spine, her body, and she molded against him.

When he traced the seam of her lips with his tongue, she parted on a sigh. He pressed his advantage, sliding inside to delight them both with the interplay of their moist muscles. Soon he found himself nibbling on her tongue before swathing the sting with his own.

She moaned and buried her fingers in his dreads, tugging on some of them just enough to fire him up as she became the assailant in their kiss.

Kaige gave her the lead. He enjoyed every bit of her aggression. She let her hands roam down his face and shoulders. A pleased hiss escaped him when she kneaded his upper arms, drawing him even closer.

In no time, they'd steamed up the windows.

His fingers wandered from her arm to the opening of her black blazer. The fitted jacket she'd replaced drove him nuts as it emphasized her tiny waist, which flared out to lushly curved hips and breasts. The instant his hands touched the bare skin on display near her killer cleavage, she froze.

"Wait."

And he knew he'd pressed his luck too far.

To avoid upsetting her, he released her, backing away slowly as if what they'd done hadn't rocked his world. No kiss had ever tasted so sweet or revved him up so fast.

Nola cleared her throat three times before she was able to say, "I think maybe we should get back to the garage."

"Sure. Your call." He didn't fight, although his heavy cock and the balls drawn tight to his groin begged him to try to persuade her for one more taste. At least. "But let me know if you change your mind… I would like to get lucky *in* my car sometime before I die."

"Gee, thanks for the open invitation. Classy." Prissy Nola reappeared.

And damn if she didn't make him harder.

Kaige was seriously fucked.

CHAPTER FIVE

When they returned to the shop, the rest of the guys had already gone upstairs, probably for dinner. "Shit. I didn't even think of how late it is."

"Me either." Nola might have resumed some of her professional shield, but the sweetness in her tone thrilled him. She didn't hide that she'd enjoyed their day—and maybe even the trip down memory lane, complete with mini-make-out session—as much as he had.

"You must be hungry." He tugged on one of his dreads. What had he been thinking? Nothing except feasting on her had entered his mind. Missing an opportunity to spend extra time with her bothered him more than his suddenly rumbling stomach. "I should have bought you dinner. We could still grab a meal."

"It's no problem. I work late a lot. Amber will have something warming on our stovetop for me." Nola crossed the parking lot in front of the service station, not shaking his hand off her arm. In those heels she was liable to break an ankle if she twisted it after stepping on one of the stray pieces of gravel strewn about.

"If you're sure…" He would have loved to invite her inside, but after the other day—and given the early closing of the garage, which usually had sparks from a blow torch lighting the place long after sunset—who knew what was going on up there.

Part of him was dying to know. Another faction shied away.

Nola had confused him when he'd finally thought he knew what he wanted.

Son of a bitch.

Didn't it figure? He'd meet a girl like her the instant he wasn't looking.

"Yeah. I'm positive. Today has been…a lot." She nodded. "So, what's the plan for this week? I have another client scheduled tomorrow, but if you definitely want me to come back…"

"I'm certain." He didn't hesitate. "As soon as you're available."

"Thursday." She smiled demurely up at him, though Kaige wasn't fooled.

Inside, she was a sizzling, passionate woman. Nola was no mouse.

"Okay." He wished thirty-eight hours or so didn't sound like forever. "I'll see you then. First thing, right?"

"Yeah." Nola unlocked her door and slid behind the wheel of her better-days Civic. Kaige stood there with one hand on the roof, his body filling the opening.

"I need to shut the door to go." She laughed and poked his thigh with a perfectly manicured nail. Mustang Sally would love to paint girly doodads on those. Hell, she probably wouldn't mind another woman around to chat with either. The lone female of the garage had been Skyping every night with the Powertools crew ladies since she'd visited Joe's construction cousin and his friends. Who happened to have a polyamorous relationship like the one the Hot Rods were forging...or had been a couple days ago.

Problem was, Kaige didn't want Nola to leave.

And that was ridiculous. They'd spent the entire day together. He couldn't remember the last time he'd done that with a woman and not gotten annoyed or longed to be home with his garagemates instead.

"I'm glad Eli recruited you." Kaige didn't give Nola a chance to object, not like she could flee since she was strapped against her car's tan cloth interior, trapped in place by her seat belt. He ducked down, swooped in and reminded her of the kiss they'd shared with a pale imitation of that scorching experience.

When she pushed lightly on his shoulder, he abandoned her with a sigh. Annoyed with himself for wanting more while she peeked in the rearview to make sure no one had seen her slumming it with him, he stepped back. "Watch your hands."

She planted them on the steering wheel, so he swung her door shut.

Nola gave a meek wiggle of her fingers as goodbye. Still, he didn't leave the lot until she'd turned the key in the ignition. The putter of her engine disturbed him. It had a hitch in the timing. And her exhaust reeked of sulfur. It needed a new catalytic converter. Pronto.

Considering the make and model of her car, he figured they could get parts from their supplier in town overnight. It wouldn't take long for him to tune her up. He couldn't help himself. He spun around in time to see her turn onto the main road.

Kaige sent her off with a wholehearted wave.

Walking backward, he waited until she disappeared out of sight, around the first curve, before jogging toward the rear of the garage and taking the stairs two at a time. He couldn't wait to talk to the guys about how he felt and the sparks they all had to have seen flying off him and Nola today. At least he hoped they could confirm his instincts. The way she flip-flopped from hot to cold had him puzzled. Could be because they'd met less than two days ago. Understandable, he supposed.

Kaige didn't mind a little thrill of the chase.

So he burst through the door into the Hot Rods' shared space. His grin sputtered quicker than Nola's engine when he realized what he'd barreled into.

Good thing he'd trusted his gut and sent Ms. Brown on her way instead of bringing her into their personal lair. What would she have said if she'd seen Eli, Alanso, Bryce and Holden each pinning one of Sally's wrists or ankles to the thick fur rug while Carver fucked her, and Roman...

What *was* he doing back there, behind his roommate?

Holy shit. Barracuda stretched Carver's ass with a finger or three as if he planned to mount their friend and ride him and Sally in tandem. Eli and Alanso sometimes liked to play like that. Kaige thought back to the carwash Mustang had orchestrated to lure them into debauchery, and how she'd tempted her pair of mechanics into nailing her on the hood of Eli's Cobra while the rest of them watched. That'd been one way to banish their inhibitions.

It'd been the first of many steps that had led them here.

Yet they still had some road to travel. He would swear the two guys had never crossed this line with each other before. Certainly the other night had seemed like a first. But would they always now? Were they a couple? Or were all of the Hot Rods fuck buddies?

Kaige's eyes grew wide and his cock leaked in his pants. After being tortured the entire day, he couldn't suffer much more without erupting. He took a step closer, encouraged by Eli's smile and the jerk of the head mechanic's chin toward the action—a clear invite to join.

Some tiny sliver of his brain that was still operational shouted to him, *Don't! Don't fuck up any chance you have with Nola.*

He was torn.

Go forward? Move back?

Hold out for a woman he barely knew, one who might never become an important part of his life no matter what his gut insisted? Or shun the friends who'd never once let him down and risk alienating himself from them?

He had nowhere safe to turn.

Welded to the floor, Kaige stood and stared. Leaving any of them with a glimmer of doubt that he approved of their progression would be impossible. He extricated his own cock—already painfully aroused by a day in close proximity to the most alluring woman he'd ever met—through the zipper of his coveralls. No way could he resist a chance at release.

Kaige stroked himself.

Alanso tipped his head, as though he might call out to Kaige, encouraging him to take his rightful place at their sides. Thankfully, Eli stopped the guy with a hand on his shoulder. Super Nova didn't know if he could have resisted another siren song leading him to temptation.

Bearing witness, yet standing apart, seemed the best compromise he could offer everyone. Including himself. Mustang Sally smiled up at him, her warm eyes too wise despite the now-familiar haze of lust and the slow, heavy blink of her lids. He'd like to think she understood.

As he stared, King Cobra reached out with his right hand and fisted Holden's dick. Swinger gasped and thrust his hips forward, poking through the ring of Eli's fingers as he made more than a handful for their leader. The rest of the guys copied the example Cobra made for them. Each mechanic stretched their free hand to their right.

Since Holden was nearest Carver and Roman, he took turns petting them, keeping them calm despite the boundaries they shattered. And Carver surprised Kaige by being alert enough as he fucked and was fucked to grasp Bryce like a lifeline, completing the circle. Soon they each jerked their neighbor while enjoying a hand job in return.

While Kaige regretted his exclusion from the unit they made, he accepted each searing look his friends leveled at him as they indulged enough for all of them. Sally's eyes rolled back as she reveled in the sweet screwing Carver gave her.

At the center of their tangle of limbs, she soaked in the passion each man expressed openly with grunts, reverent curses and the tightening of his hand on his buddy.

"Hurry, Roman." Carver looked over his shoulder. "This isn't going to last forever. I want you to come with me. With us. In me."

Alanso broke out his Spanish as they crossed into the next higher level of rapture in sync. Barracuda landed a loud smack on Meep's ass. Shit, that had to sting. But if it put the guy off, Kaige couldn't tell. Carver only plowed Sally harder and faster as the red imprint of Roman's hand began to glow across his white cheek.

"I'll tell you when I'm ready, boy." He fisted Carver's longish hair in one hand as he blanketed his roommate with his ripped body. Not an ounce of fat stuck to the guy's ribs or midsection. He humped Carver's ass, probably guiding his cock along the slick ravine between the knotted flesh, getting himself even slipperier.

"Yes, sir," Meep rasped. "But you're not making it easy. To hold out."

"Sally. Pinch his nipple for me. Kiss him while you do it, though, so he doesn't scream the house down when I fuck his tight ass." Roman said more in those thirty seconds than Kaige remembered hearing from the quiet man in the past six months.

Whoa.

When Mustang did as told, Carver stiffened between his dual tormentors. Taking advantage of his distraction, Roman guided the glistening head of his cock to the shadowed valley of his soon-to-be lover's ass.

With steady pressure, he invaded Meep. The man groaned, low and long. Barracuda's hips grew closer and closer to his roommate's ass. He backed up some then plunged forward time after time, progressing bit by bit.

"Shit, that's fucking hot." Holden caught his bottom lip between his teeth as Eli stroked him.

"Maybe you'd like to give it a try next time?" Bryce's latent promise had each of the guys glancing at him. Where was this going? How bold would each of them get?

"Highly recommend it." Roman growled through clenched teeth as he dedicated himself to making a lasting impression on Carver. He wrapped his hands around the guy's waist. Anchored, he thrust with more and more vigor until both of them sported a sheen of perspiration.

Sally absorbed any spillover energy, her body the perfect pillow for Carver. Her mewls served as excellent evidence that she loved every single second.

A spurt of precome coated the tip of Kaige's erection, allowing his fist to fly over his engorged length smoother, faster with every stroke. Eli tipped his head back and stared at the ceiling for a bit as if to cool down. Carver didn't help when he stretched to the limits in his sandwiched state to lick sloppily at King Cobra's tool.

And that was all it took.

Eli lost control. He blasted Carver, and Sally, and maybe Roman too, painting them with his hot, silky come. Kaige wondered what Nola would think of the raw beauty moments before rational thought disappeared. Like dominoes, each of the Hot Rods capitulated to desire, one by one in a ring of never-ending bliss.

Roman fucked Carver mercilessly, as if capturing each of his friends' pleasure and reinvesting it in the man beneath him. Meep twitched and groaned, inarticulate sounds that Mustang Sally absorbed the same way she took the impact of his body.

"It's okay. I won't let you go over alone." She hugged the man on top of her. "Together, all right?"

Carver moaned in response. He shuddered. Sally squeezed him tight—both with her arms and her pussy, Kaige would bet, since her echoing cries could only mean she'd surrendered to an epic orgasm. Roman gripped Carver's ass hard enough to leave bruises, though Meep wouldn't mind. Barracuda let the smaller man ride out his orgasm on the thick length of his cock before shouting at the metal rafters in their common space and unleashing his own monumental release.

A couple of the guys recovered enough to support Roman as he yielded to the moment and years of pent-up passion. Bliss pulsed through Kaige with every slam of his heart while he watched contentment blanket his friends. Nothing could make him happier.

Sally lifted her gaze to his and smiled.

Kaige shuddered as he pumped jet after jet of come from his cock. He hadn't realized he'd toed the edge so close. As if he were sixteen again, he was swept away by a massive orgasm that awed him with its intensity and the thoroughness of his ecstasy.

The only thing that could have made it better would have been pumping into Nola while he watched his friends connect with each other. If they could have shared that bond...

Another wrench of his spine pulled the last droplets from his balls.

He leaned against the couch to keep from falling on his face.

For a moment, he enjoyed the endorphin high. Then reality set in.

Instead of joining the laughing, exhausted group of friends piled on the floor, replete, he bolted. It wasn't pretty—or manly—but he didn't give a shit. Enticement too strong might make him do something he regretted. Because he couldn't ignore the energy that had travelled between him and Nola today.

Right before he got to the hallway, leading to his room, Sally's soft call had him turning toward her. "Kaige?"

"Yeah, Mustang?"

"We'll be here when you figure it out." She smiled slowly, then stretched like a sleepy kitten instead of a wild horse. "I'm not going anywhere for a long, long time. And for the record, I think she's great too. Someone I could be friends with."

"Thanks."

"Do you want to t-talk about it?" Roman shocked the hell out of him by offering to discuss what were sure to be feelings even messier than Carver's back was at the moment. From the wide-eyed glances winging between the other members of their gang, Nova wasn't the only one caught off guard. Maybe all this sharing had unlocked more than sexual aspects of their complex relationship.

"Uh—" He froze.

"It's okay if you're not ready." Sally laid her hand on Barracuda.

"I gotta sort some stuff out first." Kaige twisted his fingers in his dreads, gathering them then letting them fall again.

"Go." Eli didn't command him to his room as some kind of punishment. It was a freedom and an acceptance of their combined needs, even if that meant taking a hiatus. "Why don't you call the crew? You can say anything to them and not have to worry about stepping on anyone's toes unintentionally. Go ahead, tell them about your crush."

Bryce knocked into Holden with his elbow as both guys smirked. They approved of Nola, or they wouldn't have encouraged him like this. One hurdle jumped.

It made Kaige admit to himself without reservations that there had been something special there. An indefinable chemistry.

That's what he'd searched for his whole life. A woman who made him feel alive, smart, and special while firing him on all cylinders. Nola could be the one.

Could he risk finding his soul mate for a life of lust with his garagemates?

As much as he wanted to strengthen the ties between them, could he be happy with that camaraderie alone? Especially after seeing up close and personal the joy Eli, Alanso and Sally had brought each other once they took their relationship to a sacred place, beyond physical intimacy, or even the bestie status they'd enjoyed in the friend zone.

He took a deep breath then another, refusing to hyperventilate and black out like he had the day his mother went missing. Before he'd quite recovered, he'd perched on the cracked concrete steps of a home he never intended to return to though he had only the clothes on his back.

Could today turn out to be as pivotal as that one had been?

Kaige slammed and locked his door then hauled his laptop onto his unmade bed. He only took time to kick off his boots before shoving his shoulders against the headboard and flipping open his computer.

A text to Dave alerted the man to his need to speak. *I'm gonna Facetime you. In 3...2...*

Don't hang up. I need to go grab my tablet. BRB, came the response, which vibrated Kaige's phone.

He tossed the device onto his pillow then waited for the laptop screen to flip from blackness to a live idyllic mountain scene. Trees with bright green leaves swayed gently in the breeze. A sapphire lake at the foot of the mountains that cradled Dave and Kayla's naturist resort, Bare Essentials, came into focus.

Dave's naked chest hogged most of the screen, his massive shoulders easily stretching the full width of the frame. Guaranteed he didn't have any pants on either. The crew had embraced the lifestyle of one of their members. Kayla. Everyone brought something to the table. Something they all could share and learn from.

Maybe the same could be true for Hot Rods? Would they invite a new member into their midst after so long? Could they adapt and grow?

So many stranger things had happened at this point in Kaige's life, nudity didn't faze him. Especially not when some of the crew wives meandered across the massive deck overlooking the valley behind Dave. Super Nova figured it'd be polite to give them a heads up at least before they started getting their freak on like his own Hot Rods had done. The mechanics had learned their tricks from these sexperts. "Good evening, ladies."

Kayla and Devon turned, flashing their pretty, tanned-all-over breasts. Damn, why had he seen a bunch of people naked today, yet not the person he wanted?

"Super Nova!" Kayla waved and bounced in her excitement to see him. That did absolutely nothing to take his attention from her gently swaying tits. Except instead of imagining her or Devon welcoming him to their group, all he could picture was Nola's face instead.

Uh-oh.

"What's that look for?" Dave squinted into his laptop's camera. "I thought Eli was going to smooth things over with you? You're still pissed from a couple nights ago? I figured you two would—"

"Nah. That's not the problem." Kaige cleared his throat. Obviously someone had caught their friends up on recent highlights and lowlights.

"It's the sex. It freaked you out?" Dave's mirth rumbled across the speaker. "It's okay, it wigged Neil too the first time."

"Actually...that's not it either." His skull hit the wall harder than he anticipated when he let his head fall back. The impact rattled his brain.

"Seriously?" Kay and Devon came to sit beside their husband and friend. "How much stuff could you have going on all at once?"

"It's a girl. I met a beautiful, genius, funny, badass woman." He lifted up so they could see the truth in his eyes.

"Well, that's some timing you've got there, Super Nova." Dave chuckled. "The consultant? Ms. Brown? I take it she's not really eighty-five with horn-rimmed glasses then, huh?"

"More like smart, young and stacked." He scrubbed his eyes as memories of her flashed before them.

"Wow. You must really like her if *stacked* came last in that list." Devon snorted.

"Yeah." He wasn't laughing. "So what the fuck do I do? I have to be upfront, don't I?"

Kayla nodded. "I think you do. I knew about the crew before I went on my first date with Dave. It was shocking enough to hear then. I would have felt betrayed if he hadn't told me in the beginning."

"I sort of walked in on the crew's fun. Definitely before anything happened between me, Neil or James." Devon agreed. "She deserves to know what she's getting herself into. Because it's going to be about more than you and her. Isn't it?"

"Well. Shit. That's a big leap. I mean, I haven't even asked her out. Although, I did sort of kiss her." He couldn't smother his grin.

"Pretty sure there's no *sort of* involved when you play tonsil hockey with someone." Devon grinned. "Was it good?"

"Amazing." He sighed.

"So you're going to have to spill the beans. Talk to the guys and double check they don't mind. They won't. Then let her know how it is with you." Dave spoke slowly as he considered his advice.

"How the hell do you admit to a girl you just met that you get it on with some or all of your roommates but that you still want to find a forever woman of your own?" A headache began to throb at the base of his skull.

"She doesn't need details since you guys are still figuring it out. Tell her things are complex and dedicated," Kayla chimed in. "Most important, convince her you'd like her to be a part of what's going on regardless of what that specifically entails. You know, maybe not diving into the deep end right away but...eventually. If things worked out."

"So much for starting with a simple trip to the drive-in." Kaige shook his head.

"Well, you could go the date route." Dave scratched his chin. "Why not ask her to be your plus-one for the wedding? Maybe it's better to show her than to talk. Relationships like ours might be hard to explain, but once you witness it for yourself, it's hard to deny that it's right."

"Eli and Alanso thought so when they crashed one of our sessions." Kayla kissed her husband on the cheek. "Sally too, when we put on a demonstration for her. You're right. That's a perfect solution."

"Nola already knows about Eli, Alanso and Sally." Kaige shrugged. "She didn't seem freaked out by that. And if she is, I guess it's better to know how she feels about it before I get attached, right?"

"True, though that's not what Dave meant. He was talking about the after-party." Devon rubbed her hands together.

"What?" Kaige tipped his head but when the trio on the other end of their web conference caught his confusion, they backpedalled.

"Umm...forget we told you about that. It might be a surprise." Kayla pretended to zip her lips and throw away the key. "But damn, people should warn you something's top secret when they give you intel like that."

"You're saying..." Kaige's eyes grew wide as he speculated.

"I'm not making another peep." Dave waved his hands in front of his chest.

"Well, maybe a couple more." Devon leaned forward. "You want to bring your Nola to the wedding if you're serious about seeing what's possible. And if she runs, we'll be there to convince you she didn't deserve you anyway."

"You've got a week and a half to work your magic on her before then." Dave grinned. "Do your worst, Super Nova."

A smile spread across his face as a new sort of strategy coalesced in his mind. "I'll do that. Thank you."

"Anytime." The trio waved at him, the women blowing kisses as Dave reached forward and severed their connection.

Alone in his room, Kaige didn't feel abandoned. Friends surrounded him. A phone call or a shout away. And now he had the shot of a lifetime.

Kaige flopped onto his pillows, grinning.

Game on.

CHAPTER SIX

Kaige tightened the last of the bolts on Nola's exhaust. He probably had set a world record while swapping out her catalytic converter. Still, he ensured his work met his high standards. No way would he risk fucking up her car. After a final pass over the system, he nodded and shoved against the chassis a bit harder than he'd planned so his creeper rocketed from beneath the vehicle.

"Eager to check on your consultant?" Bryce raised an eyebrow from where he wiped his tools clean with a soft rag.

Kaige shrugged, though he couldn't possibly pull off nonchalant when Rebel knew him so damn well. Plus there was the whole email fiasco, which had made the full extent of his Nola-obsession breaking news in their apartment last night. You'd have thought it was a politician's sexting scandal by how riled the Hot Rods had gotten.

He'd been chatting with Nola again. They'd exchanged enough messages throughout the day and two nights they'd been apart to trigger his computer's spam warning.

Dumb stuff. Important stuff. Background stuff. Cute stuff. Business stuff.

He'd lost track, really, content to chat with her about anything.

At some point, he'd taken a couple empty beer bottles from his side table to the kitchen, then stopped by the bathroom to piss.

When he emerged from the tiled space, the living room had gone deathly quiet, something that almost never happened in their apartment. All seven of his garagemates huddled around the couch. At first, he thought they were going to get it on again, and he was game to watch. Then Holden snorted and Kaige knew…

"Hey," he'd bellowed as he attempted to rescue his laptop from their clutches.

But it was way too late for that.

"So *this* is what you've been going crazy over?" Swinger pointed to the special folder he'd made for Nola's six hundred and thirty-seven messages. "We thought you'd gotten sucked in to gambling online or found some extra-perverted porn or something you were hoarding on here."

"Yeah, I've seen your fuck face…and you're wearing it when you look at her emails." Alanso's revelation could have been another of their usual jabs or a real accusation, Kaige couldn't tell. Not with his heart pumping double time like his pipes were gummed up with ancient oil, or whatever caused this slick feeling in his guts.

Had he broken some unspoken pact between the Hot Rods by flirting in overdrive with Nola?

He shouldn't have worried. In the next instant they began harassing him to take things further.

"So when're you going to ask her out?" Carver had slapped Nova on the back. A wicked grin creased his face. "She's hot. And smart. Tough, too. She can probably take you."

The shadow that flashed over Bryce's face spoke of something else entirely. Would Kaige upset their balance if he acted on the attraction growing stronger between him and Nola by the minute?

He didn't have time to worry about it right then, because the guys had all chimed in, acting more like fourth graders when they teased him about his pen pal and writing notes. Sally had even piled on, asking if he'd sent one that had two check boxes after the questions, *Do you like me? Yes or no?*

It felt good to laugh with his friends. A relief to have the full extent his irrational yet undeniable feelings out in the open, as if the Hot Rods could have stayed ignorant for long. Hell, half the time he'd been slinking around the garage with a hard-on. That certainly hadn't gone unnoticed.

They made sure he knew it too.

Except then the heckling had disintegrated to wrestling, which had resulted in a broken coffee table and a pile up of an entirely different nature.

He'd observed from the sidelines as they bonded.

Now he was spinning his wheels.

Torn between the gang he belonged in.

And the girl he'd just met.

To comfort himself as he'd lain wide awake, he'd reread her witty emails a half-dozen times each before trying to top her in an equally playful response.

So what if he'd looked forward to the little *bing* of the delivery notice like a teenage girl in the throes of puppy love until he'd drifted off, still clutching his computer?

This morning Sally had given him crap when she'd caught him checking out his reflection in their stainless steel refrigerator before heading down to the shop. At least before she saw him swallow hard and realized this meant something to him. Then she'd rearranged his dreads and smacked him on the ass through his coveralls, promising he was a "sexy beast".

The day and a half since Kaige had last seen Nola had seemed like a lifetime. When she'd strolled into the shop a few hours ago in skinny jeans that hugged every curve of her willowy thighs along with a sheer blouse the color of rust, a chunky silver cuff—with a skull and lightning bolts carved into it—that dwarfed her slender wrist and a pair of beige leather heels that even Sally had drooled over...

Well, he'd nearly dropped to his knees and begged her to take the day off. With him.

Instead, he'd walked her to the temporary office and helped her set up her tablet on the shop's WiFi. They'd both agreed she had way better presentation skills than he did. So she intended to organize his strategy and jam it into a format that would allow him to show the rest of the Hot Rods, clearly and concisely, what he'd been scheming about for months.

After hovering around her for a couple minutes, and stealing one tiny peck, Kaige had gotten kicked out. Nola laughed as she told him to do some work while she got busy. What he wouldn't give to be getting busy *with* her.

He tucked his gloves in his back pocket as he ducked Bryce then appeared—he hoped—

to mosey casually toward the break room. Hell, he actually had skipped lunch to try and bang out his jobs with enough spare time to collude with Nola. Or maybe just to watch her in action. Pathetic.

"If you're looking for your lady friend, she's outside taking a break. I think she might turn into a troll if we keep her locked in that dungeon much longer." Mustang Sally poked her head out when he passed by the paint booth.

Kaige winced. He should have checked on Nola sooner instead of flying through his list of to-dos. He wandered out of his open bay, scrubbing his hands on a rag he tugged from the empty belt loop of his jumpsuit. He turned his face to the warmth of the summer sun, closing his eyes to absorb the heat and light. Not a bad idea to soak in the rays after being cramped beneath the shadowed underbelly of the beauty he'd installed a new suspension on today before playing with Nola's ride.

It had been well worth the cramps when he finished, but a timeout was in order. He took a lap around the building, stretching his legs. Okay, really searching for the one person he wanted to share a minute or two with.

There, near the storage shed, her pert ass made a hell of a reward for his efforts this morning. What the hell was she doing rummaging around in that junk though? She was likely to cut herself on something that'd require a tetanus shot.

"Nola?" He would have liked to have laid his palm on her bottom if he didn't suspect she'd bolt upright and crash into the pile of stuff waiting to be taken to the dump or get recycled.

"Oh!" Sure enough, she stood straight. Engrossed in whatever she'd been doing, she probably hadn't heard him come up from behind. Her smile was offset by the worry lines creasing her forehead. "I'm glad you're here. I was taking some pictures of the grounds for the slides on the additional outbuildings we discussed and I thought I heard something in here."

"Like what?" Kaige tilted his head and strained. No sounds reached his ears past the thumping of his heart and the rustle of leaves in the trees as a summer breeze morphed heat into something pleasant instead of unbearable.

Just when Nola opened her mouth, he caught it too. A soft whimper and some scratching.

"I think it might be a puppy. There was a tiny bark when I first came over." She dove toward the scraps, climbing on an old bumper in those hot yet completely inappropriate shoes. She'd make a fine circus act balancing precariously like that.

After a moment of envisioning her in a spangled unitard with her mile-long legs showcased, he shook his head and wrapped his arm around her waist. He lifted her to safer territory and went to investigate in her place.

"Hang on a second. You're about to ruin that blouse. Or hurt yourself. Let me." He whipped his gloves from his pocket and tugged the thick leather over his still-sore fingers. Though honestly, one more nick or scratch would hardly be noticeable.

He tipped a few things this way and that, wincing when something crashed in the far reaches of the pile.

"Careful, don't squish it." Nola leaned in. "Is there a flashlight somewhere?"

"Actually, yeah. Above the side door, near the first-aid kit." He smiled at her adorable concern. "Would you mind?"

She trotted across the lawn on her toes as if she could win a triathlon in those stilettos. Hell, Sally could hardly manage not to break her ankle walking on flat surfaces. Kaige didn't deny himself the pleasure of observing her rearview, though.

Another tiny cry had him crouching and wiggling his hand. He didn't like to think about what else might be hiding in the crack along with their newest visitor. Still he couldn't quite seem to reach whatever was inside. "Hang on, little guy. We're gonna get you out of there in a minute. I promise."

As if his voice might actually have some calming effect, the whimpers slowed down.

Nola cleared her throat from behind him. When he peeked over his shoulder, she had a funny look on her face.

"What's wrong? Couldn't find it?" He scrunched his eyes. The sun haloed her hair enough to turn it auburn instead of nearly midnight as it appeared indoors.

"No, it's just...I like the way you were talking." She flipped on the beam of light and directed it through the super contrasting shadows. "I didn't think you'd be so sensitive."

Nola squirmed. Holy crap, was she turned on by him talking to an animal?

Shit, he knew what it was like to be a stray.

He'd never leave whatever had hijacked a trip in one of their restores, or wandered out here in search of shelter, to fend for itself.

Kaige didn't answer her. Instead, he followed the sweep of her yellow light. A flash of something. Eyes. "Hang on. Right there."

A tiny puppy stared up, then blinked rapidly at the sudden change in illumination.

Dirty and thin, it wriggled against a sheet of grating they'd put in the heap a few days back. Had it been trapped all this time?

"Okay, I've got it now. Let me jiggle this a little…" He hadn't moved the metal more than a couple inches when a blob of black and once-white fur burst from its prison and cowered against Nola's ankle.

She reached her hands out as if to scoop up the puppy, who shivered and licked her, but Kaige beat her to it. The thing needed a bath. Bad.

The grime coating the furball didn't stop Nola for a moment.

She pressed close to Kaige as she inspected it for obvious wounds and found none. As concern dwindled, she fell in love right in front of Nova's eyes. Her giant heart melted all over the baby dog.

"Oh my goodness, he's the cutest thing ever." Nola patted the puppy until Kaige got kind of jealous of her gentle strokes and scratches. He'd wag his tail too if she treated him to such generous caresses.

"He's yours, then." Kaige might have developed a soft spot for a woman who took in pets without parents if he let himself. After all, he'd once been as homeless as that pup too. "I'm sure he'll adore being spoiled rotten by you."

Her face fell. The sparkle in her deep almond eyes faded a bit and suddenly he felt as though he'd kicked the bundle of energy squirming in his arms, trying to nestle against those lush breasts pressed so close. "There's no way my landlord will let me have him. He practically made me sign my firstborn over to him in my lease. Strictly no animals. 'Dogs' might have been underlined about six times."

"Ah, shit." Suddenly Kaige had the urge to make it right for her, somehow. She'd kept her head down, collaborated with him on their project and let him retain the final say about everything they drew up together. Like it or not, he respected their outside consultant.

Damn, her.

And her displaced little dog too.

Because there was only one way this was going to end.

"Well, the shop could use a mascot. Don't you think?" Kaige scratched his jaw, wondering who the hell was going to take the thing for walks and make sure it got fed. Responsibility was not his forte.

He studied the black-and-white markings on the baby beast. Lavishing the stumpy thing with attention, he worked off some of the sneaky protectiveness and the urge to coddle someone—the Hot Rods, or Nola even—that had been building in him since Monday.

What? Just because he was going to turn thirty this year didn't mean he had to get all...paternal...did it? Maybe it was the infants their Powertools friends kept flashing around every time they got the chance to brag about the rugrats. Ugh.

To prove to himself that the Kaige he knew and had come to terms with still lurked somewhere inside, he made sure to scratch behind the puppy's ears, brushing his knuckles up against the plump mounds of Nola's breasts in the process.

He wasn't sure which of the two leaned into his touch more.

Hmmm, a good sign, he thought.

"Would you guys really give it a home?" Nola aimed those big wide eyes up at him. He might have said yes to anything to make her happy.

"Let's see what the rest of the gang thinks." But he already knew what their answer would be. None of them would be able to turn away their garage crasher.

Before he and Nola made it inside, Sally emerged from the side door near her studio. She smiled when she saw them, then squealed when she realized what Kaige had cradled to his chest.

Mustang practically galloped toward them. Fast enough that the puppy quivered and burrowed deeper into Kaige's grasp, seeming more and more likely to lunge for Nola's bosom. The creature was smarter than he looked.

"Sorry, fella." Sally slowed her approach and softened her voice until she cooed. "No one's gonna hurt you here. You're safe. Look how freaking adorable you are. I could squeeze you right now."

"Try not to pop his head off, huh?" Kaige couldn't believe the sight of one mangy runt could thaw even Mustang Sally. They were doomed.

Sally's slap only reinforced his opinion of her strength. It stung a little more when Nola laughed at the abuse he took from the Hot Rod's puniest member. The two women had quickly become friends, making him wonder if they'd been exchanging some emails of their own in the past two days. He'd even overheard them chatting about going shopping together this weekend while he had been beneath one of his projects. Weirder still because Mustang Sally bitched about trips to the mall most times, at least when she had to stick to their mission-style outings. The guys went for an item then made a beeline back to their cars.

Nola and Sally sounded like they'd be missing for hours, wandering aimlessly in retail hell.

Their excitement seemed to draw a crowd. When Bryce straggled from the garage to see what was up, the puppy whimpered. For a moment, Kaige thought it was objecting to the crush of people peering down at him and wiggling their fingers in his face. As the big guy got closer and the dog made it tough to hang on to him securely, Kaige began to think maybe he feared the hulking dude.

Until a yelp from the bundle of fur startled Nola. Kaige reflexively put a hand on her back to keep her from losing her balance, but with only one hand left to secure the squirming creature, the puppy refused to be held a moment longer. He wriggled until Nova had to bend to deposit him on the grass. That or let him kamikaze dive the whole way.

With a happy bark, their new friend hopped through the tall blades right toward Bryce.

"Well, who do we have here?" Laughing, Rebel picked up the puppy and looked at it eye to eye. He examined the black-and-white markings and pointy ears of the junkyard castaway. Had someone thrown out a litter of puppies?

Kiage rubbed his chest. Nola linked her fingers through his free hand and squeezed.

The dog's miniature tail wagged like windshield wipers in a monsoon.

"I've always liked Boston Terriers. Is he yours, Nola?" The wistful stare he shot the woman by Kaige's side sealed the deal.

"No." She shrugged, dragging Kaige's linked hand along with hers when her shoulders rose. He liked her warmth and the ease with which she'd touched him.

Unafraid. Despite the glimmer of temper she'd seen slip through his control that first day in Eli's office. Could she handle one of his full outbursts? Why should she have to? Maybe he could be better for her.

"I think he's yours." Nola beamed, her bright white smile hitting Kaige in the gut. "He seems to have adopted you."

Eli, Alanso, Carver, Holden and Roman had joined them by now.

The rest of the Hot Rods talked excitedly about the possibility of an addition to their family. Except right then, Kaige was thinking of inviting someone else entirely into their midst. Could this work?

Would they welcome a woman with arms open as wide as they were for this pup?

He thought they might. The guys appreciated Nola—her hard work, her humor, her refusal to be cowed. Sally had latched on to her in a way that made him realize how short of female companionship the painter had been for years.

Not least of all, the sparks of attraction between him and the prickly consultant grew brighter by the hour.

"What's this ruckus out here for?" Tom moseyed over from his house. "Can't a guy take a nap in his hammock?"

Though he addressed the whole group, he peered between Kaige and Nola, who still held hands. Huh. Nova hadn't realized he'd never let go. And neither had she.

"I was taking some pictures for our presentation and heard an animal. Kaige rescued him." Nola beamed up at Kaige until he had to look away.

"My hero!" Holden teased as he kicked up one heel and folded his oil-stained hands like a damsel in distress.

Kaige didn't waste any time in flipping him the bird.

"It's a puppy." Rebel held out his new buddy toward Tom. "A Boston Terrier under all this mud, I think."

"Looks like." Tom nodded, smiling. Still, he glanced at Kaige and Nola more than the tiny monster, who now licked any piece of Bryce he could reach.

Alanso jogged to the hose and filled an old flowerpot for the dog. The mutt didn't wander more than an inch or two from Rebel as he drank the cool, refreshing water.

"Can we keep him?" Sally begged King Cobra.

Tom laughed. "I'll never forget when my son asked the same of me the day you wandered into the youth shelter."

"And look how well that turned out." Even Carver got in on the action, trying to persuade their boss on behalf of Bryce, who'd clearly already decided what he wanted. Kaige silently cheered for them to prevail. Then maybe Nola would come visit the bugger after her assignment was over.

"What the hell are you guys asking me for?" Eli shrugged. "It's *our* place. All of ours. If everyone wants the dog..."

"We do," Roman spoke up. Usually quiet, when he had something to say, they listened.

"Then it's settled," Eli grumbled. "But I'm not going to be the only one feeding it and walking it."

"Between us all he'll be no problem." Bryce didn't take his eyes off the puppy, who practically fit in the palm of his hand.

"What should we call him?" Kaige wondered.

"Buster?" Holden offered at the same time Sally pointed to his white feet and suggested, "Hightops?"

Everyone looked to Bryce for a ruling. He glanced between both of his friends and frowned, as if he didn't want to hurt either of their feelings. Especially now that they were getting frisky together, their bond had drawn even tighter.

Sensing the discord, Nola did what she ruled at. She solved the problem. Smoothing things over in the process. "I think Buster McHightops is the most adorable name I've ever heard for a dog."

A giant smile spread over Rebel's stubbly jaw. "It's perfect. *He's* perfect. Thank you."

Kaige never abandoned his hold on Nola's hand. Not even when his friend sidled closer and surrounded her in a quick embrace.

Could the rest of the Hot Rods like her too? As in *like* like? Oh shit, Kaige hadn't even considered that he might have competition for the woman. He didn't mind sharing, but he wanted her to be his first. He was going to have to move fast.

Ask her out. To the wedding, or something simpler.

Soon.

And maybe the energy he sensed flowing between them all could come in handy later. After he'd already staked a primary claim.

CHAPTER SEVEN

Despite his best efforts to coax her out, Nola had evaded being alone with Kaige for almost two days. Either by chance or by design, he couldn't tell. Could she sense that he intended to corner her in the hopes of pressing things beyond their professional boundaries? After the puppy fiasco Thursday, everyone had given up on work for the last few hours of the day.

On top of that, when Nola spied her car on the lift she'd been thrilled until he declined her offer to take the parts and labor out of her bill. Like hell he would.

Eventually she'd graciously accepted his help, thanking him with a kiss that could have become a lot more steamy if Buster McHightops hadn't chosen that moment to scurry between them and piss on Kaige's boot. A love/hate relationship had sprouted between him and the mutt.

Of course all the other Hot Rods had thought the antics hysterical. And while Kaige was upstairs changing, Nola had slipped away. Maybe the intensity between them had frightened her or maybe it had been the rest of her employers catching them sucking face that had shoved her out of arm's reach during business hours. Because ever since then the week had flown by with their consultant keeping her cute head buried in her laptop, pounding out the details of her presentation.

How the hell much could she be doing? Enough to warrant even coming in on the weekend to keep trucking, he supposed.

She wouldn't let him see her progress until the thing was finished. Of course, that meant she was constantly around, if out of reach behind her expert demeanor. They'd shared meals together, played with the new shop mascot, hung out near the water cooler on breaks and chatted about everything and nothing in between his jobs and her work.

At night, they continued their email exchanges. Nola was like no pen pal he'd ever imagined. It seemed as though the distance between them made it easier to talk about their pasts and their hopes for the future. In person, their discussions never took on half the weight of their correspondence.

He found he liked both sides of her. The serious professional and the vulnerable woman who understood so much about the events that had shaped him. She'd never once judged him. He believed his secrets would be safe in her hands. Something he rarely could say about people other than the Hot Rods.

By Saturday afternoon, Kaige had played it as cool as he could manage. He plopped into the shitty folding chair in Nola's makeshift office, rocked it onto its back legs, locked his hands behind his head and crossed his ankles on the table. The flash of heat her semi-covert scan inspired curled his toes in his boots.

"You're going to break your neck, fool." She seemed genuinely disturbed, despite her acerbic barb. Somehow she knew how to reach him. Just like the gang, who used endless taunts—borne of love—to communicate their concern.

"Nah. I'm not flying off to heaven until you escort me there." He reached for her fingers, which, surprisingly, she let him take.

"That's a lame line." She rolled her eyes.

"Yeah, but it still kind of worked, didn't it?" A grin tipped one corner of his lips upward.

"If it did, that only makes me lame too." Nola put her head in her free hand. "I know better than to fall for a guy like you."

"What's that supposed to mean?" The metal thudded to the floor as he sat up and leaned forward.

"You're a smooth talker. A hound dog latched on a scent. But will you tear me apart when you catch me? Will you still want me after you've won?" Her eyes grew wide in the dim interior of the room. They'd doused the lights so she could show him her finished presentation by projecting it on the white-painted cinderblock wall.

"This isn't some kind of game, Nola." He frowned. "I'm not toying with you. I'm interested, impressed and turned on every time I'm around you. Hell, even when I'm not. I've never had this kind of chemistry with a woman before. I'm sorry if I don't know how to show you that. I've never had to try before."

"You're doing fine on that count." Maybe honesty had something in its favor. When she stared into his eyes and read the genuine curiosity there, she smiled a bit—stealing his breath—before groaning. "But we have a project to finish. Come on, I'd really like you to see this. I'm kind of proud of how it turned out, okay?"

She waved her hand toward the bright square illuminating the wall.

"All right. If I behave and watch your thingy, will you go out with me? Like on a real date." He considered his options. "Work at work and fun when we're off the clock, like you want."

"That isn't *exactly* what I said."

"So compromise." He couldn't help himself from leaning in to steal another taste of her juicy lips. Whatever gloss she seemed addicted to was making him crave it too. Sweet and shiny, it tempted him to caress her mouth with his all day. He'd never get bored of this. When they finally broke apart, he whispered, "It's what *I* want."

Nola shivered. She was breathing hard against his skin.

He smiled broadly.

"Fine," she panted. "You win. Just...focus, please. We'll talk about the rest after. Don't distract me anymore either."

Kaige chuckled when she slapped his wandering hands and scooted her chair over to the left several inches with a horrendous screech of metal on concrete.

"As you wish, Ms. Brown." He folded his hands in his lap, hoping that between them and the low light his erection might escape her notice.

Or not.

She did a double take before clearing her throat as she fiddled with her computer.

Kaige decided to take that as a compliment. Patiently as he could manage— he refused to piss her off and give her some excuse to renege on their date deal—Nova waited for her to exhibit the end result of her hours slaving away in this tiny room, which had more in common with a cell than a real office. Maybe he'd see how the rest of the gang felt about letting her move her operations upstairs to their common area. At least it had decent natural light.

All thoughts of restructuring her workspace vanished when a graphic of one of Bryce's restomods zoomed across the screen followed by other projects the guys had been especially proud of. Each job had showcased something special, a component of his strategy.

She'd visually described what he'd struggled to put down on paper.

Genius.

Once idling in place, the lineup of cars glowed subtly, limned in a throbbing light timed to some kick-ass music. The Hot Rods logo flew into their midst. Flames consumed it until it glowed like the chassis of a car in the wake of his blowtorch.

"That was awesome!" He gawked at her. "How'd you do that?"

"It's my job." She shrugged. "Go ahead. Click something."

"Which one? Will it mess you up to go out of order?" Kaige hovered the mouse over the 1968 Bullitt Fastback they'd given some special attention to. He'd always loved how that project came out. So had its owner. The dude had insisted they accept a fifty-percent bonus.

"Nah. It's designed to be interactive. Viewed in any sequence." She smiled at his eagerness to explore. "The whole idea is that it takes a multi-avenue approach to get the brand to the next level. No one component is more important than the others. They go hand in hand, right?"

She'd really listened to him.

For a moment, Kaige blinked faster in an attempt to erase the sting behind his lids.

Instead of attempting to talk, he nodded.

For close to an hour, they pored through her conglomeration of his suggestions and the roadmap they'd drafted over the past week. Fascinated, he couldn't believe how she'd brought his concepts to life. Even the reconfiguration of the shop, incorporating efficiency improvements and the specialized equipment they'd need for some of the new lines, had seemed so real he thought he could stick his head out the door and see the revised layout for himself.

Hell, the garage could use someone like her to do the same for proposals to customers. Clients would be enthralled; unable to say no when they saw what butterflies could emerge from the caterpillars they'd driven in.

Hot Rods would never lose a bid with her by their sides. Kaige added another dimension to his plan.

"Well, there you have it," she declared. "The secrets to Hot Rods' continued success. I honestly believe you guys and Sally have a great shot at doubling your profits within a year."

"After seeing that, I don't doubt it either. What you did was spectacular." Man enough to admit it, Kaige continued, "I never could have shown the gang what I had dreamed up. Not in a way they could really understand. So convincingly. Like this. You're brilliant."

"You did the hard work." Nola surprised him with a quick hug. "I made it pretty, that's all."

"You're being too modest." He squeezed her back with interest. "You helped me brainstorm solutions to some of the sticking points that'd been bothering me for months. Whatever Eli is paying you, he's getting his money's worth. Thank you. Really."

"Well, that's a far cry from the glower you greeted me with Monday." Nola peeked up at him. This close he could see the pretty gold dusting on her lids and the dark liner she'd applied to her already gorgeous eyes.

"I was an idiot. It happens from time to time." Thank God she hadn't seen his temper tantrum the night before that.

They laughed together.

Leaning in, he almost broke his pact not to blur their lines anymore.

All work and no fun made Kaige a horny guy.

With a snap of his wrist, he shut her laptop. Business was over.

"So...about that date..." Suddenly he knew he couldn't make it a whole extra week to the wedding. Waffling on taking Dave's advice since Monday, Kaige had debated the merits of bringing someone so out of the loop to the most important day of his friends' life. It seemed selfish to drag her into such a complex situation, especially if Dave's helpful hints turned out to be true and the happy trio had something grand in the works to include their unconventional friends in their ceremony.

Kaige had to put Eli, Alanso and Sally first.

But he could take things a step further with Nola. Erase any doubts about how they'd mesh before worrying about fitting the new duo they'd create in with the gang. One step at a time and all.

"Yeah, about that. Where are you taking me?" She gathered up her papers, trying to act cool. Too bad the tension in her shoulders ratted her out. Nola was nervous.

Could this be as important to her as it was becoming to him?

"How about the movies? I think there's a chick flick playing at the drive-in. Mustang's been bugging Cobra and Al to take her." Kaige had overheard Sally telling Nola about it during one of their breaks this week. Both women had seemed excited by the ultra-hot leading dude.

"That sounds fun." She smiled over her shoulder. "Your car was comfy with that big bench seat. Way better than a theater. Plus we'll have the coolest ride there, I'm sure."

"So you about wrapped up here? There's probably a seven o'clock show." Kaige rose and stalked closer to her, drawing a deep breath filled with her peach scent. "We could grab some food at the diner next door before it starts."

"What? Now? *Tonight*?" She nibbled on her lip, again making him wish he could taste the gloss there.

"Why not?" He didn't care to spend another evening typing to her instead of talking. This past week had been an exercise in staying in low gear when he wanted to pound the gas to the floor and fly.

Unless...

"Do you already have plans? With someone else?" He gulped at the thought. A striking woman like her wouldn't lack for attention.

"Only if you count Amber." Nola smiled. "We usually watch some solid reality TV before bed."

Kaige laughed. "I'll try to be more entertaining than that."

"I don't know. Some of those shows are top notch." She shook her head. "Okay, fine. This is crazy, but...let's do it."

"Great." He held out his hand and led her from the room, pausing only briefly to kiss her. A promise of more to come. Getting on their way before she could change her mind took precedence over stealing an extra taste of her.

Okay, so he didn't make it halfway to his car before he needed another sample to hold him. He thought that was pretty good. After all, he didn't bend her over the hood and make love to her with the rest of the garage watching, the way he'd dreamed of last night.

Restraint. He had some.

Not much when it came to her though.

As they were buckled in and rolling out the open bay, he shouted over to Bryce, "Yo, Rebel, we're hitting the movies. See you guys later."

"Have fun, kids. Don't behave yourselves!" The big guy winked as he waved them off.

***

Kaige enjoyed every second of the ride through the bright summer evening and the easy conversation they kept while scarfing down greasy burgers. Nola seemed every bit as content as he was to take their email discussions further in person.

The professional he'd come to know gradually melted and left behind a funny, smart, sexy woman he couldn't help but imagine licking as clean as his ice cream bowl. She must have had a similar thought when she grew still and flushed while observing his efforts. Either that or his lack of manners horrified her.

Somehow he didn't think that was it.

With a smack, he finished off the last of the sweet cream, then dabbed his lips with his napkin, all proper and shit. She nearly busted a gut laughing.

The unapologetic ringing satisfied his senses nearly as much as his dessert had.

He found himself thinking the same thing again when the flickering illumination of the drive-in highlighted her strong profile. Being with her made his heart light and his smile a near-permanent fixture on his face.

He didn't even give a crap that the movie was corny. Hell, the romantic parts kind of got to him with Nola resting her head on his shoulder. She'd kicked off her shoes and curled up on the front seat of his car like a contented cat, practically purring where they nestled together.

Kaige could relate.

At least until the credits began to roll. He was about to suggest they wait until the screen had gone dark and everyone else had left for a little encore of their own when something pinged off the rear quarter panel.

His head whipped around and he shot from the Nova so fast Nola sprawled on the green leather. A gaggle of teenagers sat off to the side, acting like they didn't know about the fucking nick in his pristine paint job. Except their twitching and inability to look in his direction as he approached gave them away.

"Which one of you punk bastards threw a rock at my car?" He crossed his arms and spread his feet, unwilling to acknowledge that he'd been far more of a shit than them when he was their age. "I could take a chunk out of *your* hide."

Rage bubbled in his veins.

He forced himself to infuse logic into the chaos, not that successfully.

They didn't know how much the machine meant to him. How much hard work had gone into lovingly restoring the Nova from the ground up. Kaige's brain understood that, but his instincts roared at him to teach them a lesson.

In the end, he didn't have to. When faced with his ferocious snarl and the bulging muscles of his crossed arms, covered in tattoos, the pricks realized they'd fucked with the wrong guy. They hopped on their bikes and rode off in a cloud of dust.

Their sudden departure left him standing there like a loser grown-up who ought to know better than to threaten kids. Hell, they'd probably peer pressured the littlest one into the prank. He knew what that was like too...having to do things you shouldn't to keep from getting your ass beat.

A gentle hand squeezed his shoulder. "I'm no expert, but it doesn't look too bad. I bet Sally can fix it tomorrow. Right?"

"Ah, fuck." He scrubbed his hands over his face. Ashamed of his short fuse and the way he'd snapped like the section of fifty-year-old plastic trim he'd tried to salvage this morning. "I'm sorry about that, Nola. I should know better than to holler at some pimply-faced teenagers. I'm a grown fucking man. I could squash them like bugs."

"You didn't. Although they deserved it for what they did. Maybe they'll think twice about daring each other to do something so stupid again." She had a way of rationalizing that helped him deescalate. Funny, too, that they should think something so similar.

Or not, since she really seemed to understand him.

Usually people told him he was wrong to get angry, which only spiraled his sense of injustice higher and outraged him more.

"Come on, don't let them ruin our date. Sit with me." She led him to the car and crawled in first, giving him a spectacular view of her denim-clad ass.

Settling beside her, he let the red mist settle from his vision as Tom had taught him to do.

The stroking of her hand on his thigh helped a good bit too.

Well, it fired him up, but in an entirely different way.

"You didn't hurt them. Just barked enough to scare the shit out of them." She shrugged. "Probably a good lesson to learn before they come across someone with less self-control than you have."

Kaige laughed his ass off at that one. "You have no idea. I'm not good at keeping my lid on. They got lucky tonight."

"Have you ever hurt someone when you got angry?" She tipped her head as she studied him.

"Like thrown a punch? Sure. At the Hot Rods when we were younger. We'd scuffle all the time. A couple bar brawls here and there." He shrugged. "Got arrested once for clocking a guy who'd shoved his girlfriend into my car in a parking lot. She cut her head open on the side mirror. And I think he might have raped her if we hadn't come along. I should have held him for the police, but I couldn't stop myself from teaching him what it was like to suffer someone's fist."

The woman had reminded him of his mother. And the man had mimicked his father's poor treatment. There'd been no holding back. A night in the slammer had reminded him that he didn't plan to end up there permanently. Fortunately, the cops had listened to Tom's pleading on his behalf and had set him free the next morning.

Everyone seemed satisfied with that.

Not one of his proudest moments either.

"No, I get that stuff." She shrugged. "Typical guy shit, mostly. Unless you're telling me you beat someone to a pulp with a baseball bat and put them in the hospital or something."

Not yet. He'd wanted to a few times.

"Jesus." He shuddered. "No. The guy I told you about had some world-class shiners and a missing tooth, though."

The things he imagined sometimes when angry were horrible. Was that normal? He didn't think so. But he was afraid to tell even his closest friends, or Tom, about the evil hiding inside him. A gift from his biological father.

"So what's this about?" Nola laid her fingers on his pulse, then rubbed the tension from his shoulders.

And before he knew what lie he'd concoct, he'd blurted his darkest secrets. "I'm pretty sure my dad killed my mom. I have a temper. Like him. They don't call me Super Nova for nothing. I can't stand the thought that someday I could slip. Go too far and do...that...to another human being."

Huge rasping breaths sawed from his lungs. Would she run now? She should.

"Kaige, look at me." Instead of putting distance between them, she closed the gap. Cupping his chin—covered in five o'clock shadow—in her palm, she turned his face toward her. "If your dad did that... God, I can see it in your eyes. You truly believe he did."

He nodded tightly. "My father. Not my dad. Tom is my dad."

"You're *nothing* like the man who created you." She kissed him gently, leeching the last of his fury from his lips. She devoured his pain and anger, replacing it with desire and comfort. After a while, she climbed into his lap, straddling him on her knees so she could peer directly into his eyes. "Hey. I may have only known you a little while, but that's enough to be sure. Okay?"

"I guess." He didn't concede easily. Not when he'd lived with the fear for ages.

"Don't lie to me. We can work on it, but only if you tell me the truth." She rubbed her thumb over his knuckles.

In years past they might have been bruised and bloodied after an altercation. Either by him pounding the offender or some inanimate object afterward. Hell, hadn't he done exactly that on those poor tires last weekend? Faint proof of that scuffle lingered.

He needed an outlet.

But had it been shame that had kept him from acting like a barbarian in front of her or had she counteracted his vile nature with her sweet one? He wasn't sure. And maybe it didn't matter if the end result was the same.

"I worry that it's in my genes. That someday I could snap, like he did." A sigh buffeted her hair away from her softly rounded face. He hadn't realized how tightly he'd bottled that nightmare inside.

"You won't." She petted him all over, settling him even as she roused another animal instinct. "Come on, Kaige. That's not how it works. I'd bet your pitiful excuse for a father hit your mom loads of times before he crossed that ultimate line. Didn't he?"

The memory of flashing police lights and medical workers that only provoked a more violent outburst later appeared front and center in his mind. He nodded.

"You're never going to get there. If you want to hone your anger management skills, there are lots of people who can help. I'd be more than glad to go with you to meet with one of them." She kissed him again. "And I know some other fine ways to blow off steam."

She began to unbutton her blouse.

He glanced around and realized they occupied the only car left in the enormous lot. He swallowed hard. The stadium lights made a clunk as they were switched off, pitching them into darkness broken only by the soft glow of the specialty dash lights.

Startled, Nola jerked. Her ass hit the horn.

Before he knew it, they were both laughing as he tumbled her sideways into the seat he'd shoved all the way back earlier, to give them more room. He covered her, loving the way her long, lean body fit beneath him. She spread her legs, giving him the perfect place to rest, surrounded by her warmth.

Kaige descended, his mouth plying hers as his hands roamed across every inch of her that he could reach. From her toned arms he wandered upward until he cupped her breast in his left hand. Kneading, he absorbed her resulting moans and ground his cock against her mound.

She'd worked her shirt open enough that her bronze skin shone in the combination of moonlight and the glow of the dash. He kissed his way down her long, graceful neck to her collarbones, pausing to lick the seductive indentations there.

Startled, he realized what he'd originally thought was the edge of a black lace bra was actually ink. "You're tattooed too?"

A few blinks later, she registered his question. "Oh. Yeah. Not like you. I have a few simple ones. Places I can cover with my clothes."

"What's this?" He nudged aside the cup of her bra to investigate.

And didn't like what he found.

A man's name—Steven. On her chest. Over her heart.

He didn't realize the growl echoing through his car came from him until she laughed. "Calm down, Nova. It's a memorial tattoo."

"For who?" He gentled his touch on her soft skin.

"*My* dad." She swallowed hard.

"Ah, shit." Kaige kissed her again, more tenderly this time. "I'm so sorry, Nola."

"It was a long time ago." As if that dulled the pain.

He knew some hurts lingered a lifetime. Maybe he could bring her a sliver of joy. She deserved it. Hardworking and compassionate, who was there for her? Her sister and her mom.

Nova wanted to be added to that short list.

"Let's forget about the past. Both of us." He nuzzled their noses together even as he insinuated one thigh deeper between her knees, pressing the flexed muscle there against her pussy. She lifted her pelvis to enhance the contact.

"Yes. Please." She strained her neck to claim his mouth once more. How long they distracted each other with the parrying of their tongues and fingers buried in each other's hair, he didn't care. Connecting with her, like this, erased everything but how good she could make him feel.

When she began to shake beneath him, he knew that prolonging their make-out session forever would be cruel. She needed more from him and he was willing to grant her wishes. He resumed his explorations, suckling on one of her breasts then the other, while allowing his hands to keep the side of her chest he didn't feast on company.

Nola planted her feet on the seat and arched upward, granting him better access. He obliged her silent demands, tugging her bra lower until her tits were fully revealed to him. Plump yet a reasonable handful, he couldn't imagine her more perfect any other way.

Teasing her nipples between his teeth, he fluttered his tongue against the tips, making her writhe and call out his name. Her neat fingernails scored his back before her hands slipped beneath his shirt and raked his skin on her journey upward. She clasped him tight to her with both those sharp crescents and her legs, which had twined around him.

As much as he longed to rip his jeans open and plunge inside the moist heat perfuming his car, he shoved aside those base urges and committed himself to taking care of Nola. There'd be time enough for full penetration some other night. When he wasn't contorting her like a pretzel in his car with no more class than the teens he'd run off.

Kaige slipped his hands beneath her arms and hoisted her so her shoulders rested on the door and he had more space to maneuver. He glided along her body, opening the button and fly on her jeans in less time than it took his car to go zero to sixty.

Tight, the fabric resisted his attempts to divest her of it. But the combo of her rolling those killer hips and him tugging, meant they triumphed over her sexy pants. With them around her ankles, she spread her knees.

And Kaige couldn't wait a moment longer.

He lunged between her legs, burying his face against the wet spot that dampened the crotch of her elegant panties. Instead of wasting time peeling them off her or ripping such a cock-hardening garment, he left them in place, sliding the crotch to the side so he could admire the moist folds of her trimmed pussy.

"You going to stare at it all night? Or are you going taste me?" She sassed him as she observed the pure desire that had to be glowing in his eyes.

Just for that he took his time, inching toward his prize. Her howl of frustration had him chuckling against her outer lip when he intentionally began off center, away from her most sensitive flesh. Gradually he spiraled inward, skimming her clit at the top of each circular track he traced with his tongue.

Nola let him play for a bit, but she eventually caved, jammed her fingers into his dreads and used the grip to direct him to where she needed his touch most. Hard as the aluminum alloy they stamped parts from, Kaige didn't give a shit if she saw him grind his cock against the seat while he devoured her.

Lapping her slit from the base to the apex, then swiping sweet cream from around her clit, he made sure she knew he preferred the taste of her to the dessert he'd inhaled earlier. Working two fingers inside her tight sheath, he savored each of her pretty cries, echoed by the clenching of her body.

And when he pumped in and out of her in long, liquid glides made easy by the natural lubrication she supplied, Nola began to tremble. Kaige lifted his gaze long enough to witness her head thrown back as she cupped her own breast and squeezed the nipple harder than he would have done.

Nola wouldn't be an easy lover. Not some fragile flower he had to temper his lust around. No, she could handle him. And match every bit of his passion with her own.

He couldn't wait until he could sink into her. Shower her with ecstasy and prove that they were a perfect match. In and out of bed.

But what would she think if she knew how he liked to play with the rest of the Hot Rods? Would she let him show her off to his friends? Would she understand that he prized her, was proud of her beauty both of form and soul?

Did she have enough ardor to share?

He would bet she did.

Kaige imagined his buddies helping him delight the woman he was coming to care too much about. The thought of Bryce filling Nola in tandem with him resulted in a spurt of precome dampening his pants.

And when Nola surrendered to his handiwork, coming apart as she rode his face, painting him with the proof of her rapture, he nearly joined her. To hell with control or his pride.

Prepared to finish himself, he anchored Nola through the storm of her ecstasy. He used his free hand to shove open his jeans. She surprised the hell out of him when she slid to the floorboard—still spasming—and encouraged him to sit, with one leg on either side of her luscious body.

Before he could tell her reciprocation was unnecessary, she'd hummed her approval and licked his frenulum piercing then taken his cock deep into her throat and began to bob over the stiff length. One of her hands disappeared. Out of sight, she made sure he understood what she was doing with moans and cries of extended pleasure that only enhanced the manipulation of her mouth and tongue along his shaft.

Holy shit.

He grabbed for her free hand, entwining their fingers. Speech became impossible, but she didn't need him to warn her of his impending explosion when her mouth was full to overflowing with his bulging cock, which leaked faster after each pass of her lush lips.

As if going down on him really got her off, Nola moaned. She looked up at him, her mouth stretched into an impossible O around him. Her eyes rolled back and she convulsed. Taking him to the root, she managed not to bite him as she came again.

Nothing could have stopped him from joining her then.

Kaige's release railroaded him, flattening him as if a car had dropped from one of the lifts, right on top of his helpless body. His balls drew tight and launched jet after jet of semen into her mouth. She swallowed greedily, drawing every last drop from him.

When they both went limp, with her head lying on his thigh, and him petting her thick mane, he couldn't believe how wrecked he felt inside. As soon as he could coordinate his limbs, he lifted her from the floorboards and gathered her to his chest. He tucked her close to his heart and rocked them both, wondering how the fuck he was going to make things right.

For them.

For the Hot Rods.

Without speaking, they cleaned each other up and restored their clothes to some semblance of order. Instead of going out of their way to return to the shop, he volunteered to take her home since her sister had to come out to the wedding site in the morning anyway. Holding hands when he was in between shifting gears, they rode through the night to her house in a comfortable silence, each keeping their own counsel.

Overwhelmed with joy and a healthy dose of fear, he didn't try to talk, knowing he'd probably only fuck up the amazing evening they'd shared. Content, he squeezed her fingers as he pulled over where she indicated on her street. The modest neighborhood held small single-family homes with neat yards.

Kaige walked Nola to her door and laid his mouth against hers. They engaged in a sensual, seductive dance of lips interspersed with a few good ass squeezes by both parties. When they broke apart, he rested his forehead on hers and smiled.

"Good night, Nola."

"Night." She touched her swollen lips.

He walked backward a little ways before he drew enough oxygen into his lungs to think straight. "Hey, Nola?"

"Yeah?" She sounded at least half as rocked as he had been. Good.

"Will you be my date for Eli, Al and Sally's wedding?"

"You haven't asked anyone else yet?" She squinted at him. "Why not?"

He shrugged.

If he were being completely honest, none of the guys were planning to bring dates. Except him. He'd been plotting for nearly an entire week now.

"I'd love to go with you." She ducked her head as she smiled. "I've been kind of wishing you'd invite me. I didn't want to get my hopes up, though."

"Seriously?" He paused.

"Uh-huh." She hugged herself. "I've seen the stuff my sister's working on and now, knowing all of you, I'd really enjoy attending. Plus, of course, being with you. Ugh. I'm pathetic."

Kaige couldn't stop himself from jogging back to her side at her adorable admission. He kissed her hard then lifted her, whirling her around in circles. "It's going to be a hell of a good time. Especially with you by my side."

After a few rotations, she shoved his shoulders while laughing. "Okay, okay. The whole world's spinning, Nova."

"Yes, it is. And it's beautiful." He relented, lowering her to the ground slowly enough to torture them both. One last kiss and they were reluctantly prying themselves apart then widening the chasm between them again.

He crossed his legs and leaned against the hood of his car while she ascended uneven steps to her front door. When the frosted glass opened and warm light spilled onto the concrete stoop, Kaige heard a woman who could only be Nola's sister, judging by their similar voices, say, "That looked better than chocolate! You lucky cow."

"Shhh...he can probably..."

Kaige cupped his hands around his mouth as he shouted, "Yeah, I heard that. And you're right, Amber. It *was* killer. Good night to both you lovely Ms. Browns."

"Get the hell outta here." Nola was laughing as she popped her head through the doorway once more. "Go home, Nova."

"Yes, ma'am. See you Monday. I won't take it too personal if you have that stick jammed up your ass again when we're at work." He grinned when she waved then slammed the door.

Kaige sang along with every pop ballad he heard on the drive home.

As long as the rest of the Hot Rods didn't witness his ridiculous off-key karaoke, they couldn't give him shit for it. Right now, he wouldn't even care if they did.

Chapter Eight

The next week crawled by. Filled with more of the same—lots of time spent with Nola and none of it alone. The garage had gone completely insane. Chaos ruled. They were doubling up on shifts, working late into the night to clear the weekend for an unprecedented two days when the shop would remain closed during their celebration.

Extra clients demanded service, stress piled up and a puppy ran amok on top of it all.

Not to mention the pre-wedding shenanigans that kept erupting. Thank God for Nola's sister, Amber, who fought most of the fires. Everyone pitched in when needed. Kaige included. Of course that meant no more nookie, or almost-nookie even.

Though he'd gotten good at stealing kisses from Nola.

By Thursday morning, she didn't seem to mind when he tugged her into his lap for a hug in front of the guys. Hell, she'd even straddled him and dropped a kiss on his lips when he'd rolled out from one of the cars he slaved over. The maneuver had inspired wicked daydreams of getting her greasy that had made it hard for him to concentrate the rest of the day.

That might have been his downfall.

Because after lunch, a weasely middle-aged guy Kaige had done work for that morning returned to the shop, citing a damaged part. As usual, Bryce handled the complaint. The guy was great at diffusing ugly situations. He had a sophistication sometimes that made Nova curious about where Rebel had picked up those tricks.

Lord knew the man wouldn't spill voluntarily. There had to be some horrendous skeletons in his closet to keep his lips zipped in the face of everything the rest of the Hot Rods had shared.

Bryce strode from the office. His cheeks were flushed and his fist curled by his side. Wow, that dick must have pushed some major buttons to draw that much reaction from the big guy.

"What's up, Rebel?" Kaige had a sick feeling in his gut.

"Did this customer ask you to install an aftermarket ROM chip in his engine control unit this morning?" He jerked his head toward the client.

"Yeah, in addition to some other stuff." Kaige wiped his hand on his towel. "Is he bitching 'cause I wouldn't? It wasn't designed for his model. It would have overclocked the engine. I told him I couldn't do it once I got it back here and researched it. We went ahead with the other mods, but he was kind of ticked at me."

Nova shrugged. He didn't give a fuck if the dude didn't like it, he wasn't about to ruin the guy's car because he was a moron who didn't understand engineering and mechanics.

"Well, it looks like he decided to plop it in there himself after he got home." Rebel shook his head.

"Blew the engine?" Kaige let his head hang. "What an idiot. And now he expects us to fix it?"

"Worse. He says you did it." Bryce huffed.

"What!" Nova's signature anger began to surface. He swallowed it down. "You know I wouldn't do something so dumb."

"Yeah. So let me see the revised invoice where he signed off on the reduced scope of work." Rebel cleared his throat. "The copy up front still shows the chip install on the list we charged him for."

Kaige's stomach bottomed out. He'd turned in all his paperwork.

If the bill didn't reflect the changes they'd agreed to, he'd failed to have the douche initial on them.

Motherfucker.

They'd be on the hook for the entire engine.

Bryce took one look at his face and winced. He feathered his fingers through the short hair on either side of his skull. "You forgot?"

"Sorry, Rebel." How could he have messed up like that? "I'll make it right."

"It's not—" His friend was probably about to reassure Nova, for what little good it would do.

Nola chose right then to sashay into his bay. "Well, looks like I finally caught you taking a breather. You've hardly quit for a moment today."

She made a big mistake, not sensing the tension rolling off of him or maybe trying to appease it by wrapping him in a gentle hug despite the state of his coveralls.

The combination of his temper and the pent-up lust he'd harbored for days didn't do either of them any favors. Grabbing her wrists, Kaige succumbed to the emotions rioting inside him. He pinned her to the garage wall then kissed the shit out of her. He had to do something to make this sludge in his gut go away. It was this or kick that dishonest fucker's head in.

Her skull made a dull thump on the cinderblocks. Stiff arms resisted his hold, but he didn't set her free. He couldn't despite her lack of response. Had he simply startled her, or was his consuming passion—an alternate outpouring to temper—scaring the shit out of her?

Some selfish part of him didn't care. He needed this. Her.

A startled squeak exposed her shock as he prodded apart her lips.

"Kaige." Bryce had his back. "Settle down, Nova. You're being too rough with her. She didn't do anything. And neither did you. It was a mistake. Karma will get that shithead. We'll make it right. It's okay."

Shamed mixed with Kaige's fury. He released Nola so quickly, she crumbled to her knees. Or would have, if Rebel hadn't caught her, cradling their consultant against his broad chest. Seeing her dazed and shaking in Bryce's arms made Nova's stomach roil.

What had he almost done? Would he have been able to stop or give her time to process his aggressive passion if Rebel hadn't been there to apply the brakes for him?

Nova wasn't sure.

All because he'd gotten pissed at an asshole, cheating customer.

Well, really, at himself for leaving any doubt that the guy could be telling the truth.

He knew the protocol. Take pictures. Sign off on the items to be completed. Make sure to get John Hancocks on any changes to the plan.

But he'd been preoccupied with wrapping up quick and hanging out with Nola. He'd let his partners down and it would cost the shop five grand at least. Nova would make sure Cobra took it out of his pay. No reason they should suffer for his stupidity.

"I'll handle things. Cool off, Nova." Bryce jerked his head toward the back rooms.

Kaige stormed to the rear of the garage and smashed through the metal door into the walk-in storage closet across from Mustang Sally's paint booth. He needed a few minutes of peace and quiet to shove the monster back into its cage. To chain it up tight.

His fists encased the metal supports of the shelving. He relished how they dug into his palms to distract himself from the failure spurring his fury. Letting the Hot Rods down was the one thing he never wanted to do.

Yet he had.

A soft rap came on the door before someone joined him then closed it gently. From the click of heels—which came closer and closer—it could only be one person in the garage today. Nola rested her fingers on his shoulder. He'd know that touch anywhere, had come to crave it.

The fresh peach scent wafting around him confirmed her identity.

"Don't fucking touch me. Get the hell out of here." Kaige pivoted, practically shouting in Nola's face. The woman didn't have enough sense to flinch.

"You think you scare me?" She laid a palm on his cheek.

"I should." He narrowed his eyes at her bravery, which crossed the line into foolishness. "I can't be trusted."

"You can too." This time she added her other hand to his heaving chest. Everywhere she touched a coolness spread from her to him, dousing some of his red-hot ire. "The fact that you're worried means you aren't going to give in. If I've learned anything about you, it's that you're stubborn as an ass."

"That's not for certain." He hated the heat staining his cheeks.

"It is. You're hardheaded." A smile lit her face.

"That's not what I meant, Nola." The circles she talked around him made him dizzy, distracting him from the crescendo of rage he'd suffered only a few moments before.

"I know. But remember what we talked about the other night? I still believe that you're different from your sperm donor." When she leaned in closer, tipping her head back as if for a kiss, he couldn't believe she meant what it looked like she offered. "So why not channel that emotion into something positive?"

"What?" He shook his head, trying to think through the anger, and now the desire building on top, feeding off his heat.

"Come on, Kaige." She rubbed against him from shoulders to toes. Her long, lean body enticed him to call her bluff. No way could she mean it. "Use me. Burn off the bad stuff, like oil floating on water. It'll be cool and clear beneath. And fun in the meantime. Better than sulking or beating yourself up in here. I've been wondering what it'd be like to have you inside me. Your cock this time instead of just your fingers. Don't tell me you haven't imagined it too."

Nola was every wet dream he'd ever had come to life. Sexy. Confident. Capable of handling him and then some. At least on a normal day. Not now. Not like this.

"I wouldn't be able to treat you like you deserve. I'd be rough. Crass. I might hurt you." He paused their stream of kisses, gasping against her lips with his forehead resting on hers.

"Who said I need delicate touches all the time?" She clawed at his coveralls, drawing the zipper down his chest slowly.

"This is a horrible idea." He batted at her hands though not with much conviction. It was hard to stop her when he needed to touch her so badly.

"I think it would be an amazing remedy." She winced. "Except I don't have any protection with me."

"Oh." Kaige should lie. The wild part of him, still loose and charging, wouldn't allow it. "That's not a problem."

She dug in his pocket, fishing for his wallet.

"Not there." He reached up to the third shelf, rapidly allowing his better sense to be drowned out by her insistence. "We keep a stash on hand."

Nola didn't respond when she saw him whip a condom from the bin beside the vats of petroleum jelly—Sally's sick sense of humor at work. Instead she pounced.

She snagged the rubber from him before stripping his coveralls from his shoulders.

Shoving at the stained fabric, she had it bunched around his ankles in no time with his briefs only a few seconds behind. He stepped out of them, leaving his boots and his wife beater on.

Before he could whisk her sundress off, she'd ripped open the package and taken his dick in hand, rolling on the condom without any hesitation. He hated that he wondered how much practice she'd had at that. Not because he was a judgmental prick, but because he still shook and he dreaded hurting her.

Experience might help her handle his sometimes rough touches. With the rest of his gang around, he already found himself struggling to rein in the amplifying effect of their presence. If she didn't get off on this as much as he did, he'd never forgive himself.

Still, he wasn't wasting any time to argue when she sank to her knees and turned around, flipping her skirt up then yanking her ridiculous excuse for panties to the side in an invitation he had no hope of declining. The rounded globes of her ass begged him to spank them, turning the deeply tan skin there into the darkness of an overripe berry.

He might have done it too, if he trusted himself that much.

Nola rested her head on her folded arms, spread her knees and looked back at him. "What are you waiting for?"

The shard of doubt that sparked in her gaze speared him in the heart. He refused to allow his drama to impact her. No, he'd give her what she asked for and satisfy himself in the process. Already he'd forgotten about the asshole that had sent him to this purgatory in the first place. It didn't matter when she was here, like this, offering herself to him.

Kaige dropped to the floor, not caring about the hardness that smacked his kneecaps. He stopped to nip at her thighs, scenting her before he curled over her back, smothering her with his form. Hoping she knew that he planned to protect her always. One of his arms snaked beneath her, holding her up and in position as he aligned his cock with her dripping pussy.

He shouldn't have worried that she might not be ready.

What could have been an aggressive position turned into something entirely different than he envisioned when he hugged her to him, treasuring her for erasing his ugliness and making him feel as though he might still be desirable in her eyes.

Flaws and all.

With as much care as he could muster, though less than she deserved, he introduced his cock to her a few inches at a time. When he had trouble advancing, he paused, allowing her to adjust. Nola had none of that. She rocked backward, insinuating him deeper.

"This is really what you want?" He growled in her ear, using his free hand to wrap around her neck loosely. To steady her and also because it simply felt...right.

"God, yes, can't you tell? How hot does a girl have to be for you to notice?" She tried to bite his hand when he hesitated.

"Oh, I got the message." His cock reared inside her as he began to fuck. She was every bit as sultry as he'd envisioned each night he'd jerked off to fantasies of her. No woman had ever held him so perfectly.

She clutched him tight within her, massaging the full length of him with her body.

"That's right, give it all to me. Work it out. I can take it. I can handle you. Make it stop eating you alive. Fuck me, Kaige. I love it." She moaned loudly when he ramped up the pace of his thrusts. "Give us both what we need."

Her stream of talk—well, shrieking really—only turned him on more. So what if the rest of the garage could hear her begging? The possibility only fired him up.

Maybe one day the Hot Rods would see this in person.

Help him escort her beyond her limits, grant her boundless pleasure. The thought had him high on her. And every bit of arousal that increased in him snuffed more of the fury. It'd always been that way. Except he'd never been this excited before, this attracted to someone.

Nola's capacity for smothering his rage seemed infinite.

His anger was no match for her passion.

Fuck yes. His hands drifted from her neck to her shoulders then downward to her hips. He gripped her tight and drove into her again and again. Soon they were both grunting. Her knees had to ache from the concrete floor—his certainly did—and yet she met him pound for pound, impaling herself on his straining cock as vigorously as he slid it into her.

Would she hate him later for not being suave?

Especially their first time, he'd wanted to be...not this person.

"Don't stop now. Need it. Been dying for this. Quit thinking and fuck me." She reached behind her and yanked at him. Hauled off and sank her nails into his bulging forearm.

Without conscious thought, he made a similar declaration, nipping her neck even as he cupped her lush breast in one hand and used it to anchor them while he rode her.

It wouldn't be some long, drawn-out affair. Not this time around.

He'd make it up to her later. He promised them both silently as he tunneled in and out of her silky sheath. Nola's flesh gloved him.

Kaige didn't need to worry. When he gave in to the urge to pinch the nipple poking his palm, Nola shuddered in his arms. She quaked around him and came in a climax so epic the undulation of her pussy tugged him along with her into orgasm.

They might have tried to be quiet, but their cries of completion echoed off the nonporous surfaces of the storeroom. Together, they crashed to the floor, laid full out, with him attempting to keep from crushing her by supporting himself on quivering arms.

At the moment, he couldn't say he gave a flying fuck about their vocal performance. Though maybe Nola wouldn't want the whole world to know she'd let him screw her in a glorified closet.

Doubts began to erase his satisfaction.

Until she rotated in his hold, coming to rest face up beneath him. The sleepy kitten look on her face went a long way toward reassuring him that he hadn't totally ruined his chance for a decent first impression. Damn if he didn't hope to do this again soon.

"Are you okay?" He traced a purple mark on her collarbone. Unlike Sally's porcelain skin, it'd take a fair bit to show on Nola's shaded complexion. Had he gone too far after all?

"Amazing. The things your piercing does in that position should be illegal." She moaned then drew his hand to her mouth and kissed his fingers.

"I didn't hurt you?"

"Hell no." Nola licked her lips.

"Totally freak you out?"

"Only if you count being completely caught off guard by how great that was. I've never come so hard in my life." She hummed as an aftershock racked her body.

"Are you su—"

"Kaige, quit the fusspot act before I start to think you assume I'm weak." The Nola he knew and adored surfaced. He could imagine her putting her hands on her hips over her rumpled dress, if she'd been able to move.

"You?" He laughed. "Never."

"It's my job to analyze situations and figure out root problems." Nola sat against the cinderblock wall, toying with one of his dreads. Content to let her pet him, he merely nodded his agreement. Until she surprised him with her insight. "Every time I've seen you lose your temper, it's because you think you've disappointed someone you love. Eli, Hot Rods..."

She didn't name herself from the debacle that had interrupted their date and shown his true colors, but Kaige would have in her place.

Would she freak at such a bold proclamation? Because lovers or not, he knew she'd earned a place in his life that wasn't temporary.

"I think when you admit that letting people down is the thing that scares you most, it won't have the power to send you into this frenzy anymore." She didn't give him time to object. "Don't you trust your friends to love you unconditionally? Don't you believe that you deserve them?"

"Uh—" Maybe some part of him worried that if he fucked up they'd disown him. Even after so long together. He tried to sit straighter, but Nola kept him pinned to her with her deceptively strong arms. His cock twitched despite the way she'd wrung him dry not five minutes ago.

"Everyone fucks up, Kaige." She squeezed him tight. "No one's perfect. Hell, Rebel has that bug up his ass about rich people. He's reverse classist and pretty rude about his prejudice. Honestly, I have no idea how he manages to hide it when he works customer service. But you guys still accept him, including his faults."

"You like him too." Kaige was quick to defend his friend, proving her point he supposed. "If you didn't, you wouldn't have let him keep Buster McHightops."

"True." Nola smiled down at him. "I think he's adorable. A big, sweet lug. Even more so now that he's got that puppy following on his heels."

This time Kaige couldn't keep his boner down. Because an image of Nola sandwiched between him and his best friend flashed into his mind. What if she was down with sharing?

No way, she'd never…

Would she?

A loud bang on the door startled them both. Nola yanked the skirt of her sundress down, covering her perfect thighs, now enhanced with several love bites he hardly remembered administering before he'd mounted her.

Kaige cursed as he levered himself to his feet. He drew on his jumpsuit, hopping from one foot to the other and barely closing the zipper before cracking the door.

"Wanted to make sure you two hadn't killed each other." Mustang Sally peeped through the gap, swiping paint speckles from her fingernails. Her wide eyes took in Nola's disheveled state. "From my studio, it sounded like two wounded animals fighting in here. The fact that I could hear you over the compressor is pretty impressive."

Instead of shying away, Nola came to the door, opening it completely. "Thanks, Sally. I'm fine. *Reeeeeeeeally* fantastic in fact."

The women high-fived each other, then hugged.

"You're good for our Super Nova. Yeah, you are." Mustang Sally whispered, "Thank you."

"How do you feel about telling your future husband that we're taking the rest of the afternoon off?" Kaige wasn't about to let what had happened slip away. He needed to talk to Nola. In private.

Despite being afraid, maybe it was time to come clean about the extent of the Hot Rods' relationship. Losing her now would be easier than getting dumped in a few months when he could no longer hide the bond the gang of mechanics shared. It would come out sooner or later.

She wouldn't appreciate being lied to.

Or cheated on. Because they weren't just fucking around anymore.

But keeping his hands off the Hot Rods was killing him too. The ruckus echoing down the hall from their common area at night nearly had him howling at the moon. He felt stuck, not fully making anyone happy—Nola or the gang.

Flickers of irritation prickled the nape of his neck. Maybe Nola was right about that. Because right now he felt like he was disappointing everyone.

Himself included.

"I'll cover for you." Sally winked. "If I do it right, he won't even notice you're gone."

"I owe you." He kissed Mustang's forehead, then hauled Nola to his car.

Though he thought they might talk and get around to trying sex again, except a variety more mellow this time, they actually ended up taking a nap together. Snuggled in his car, they parked in a field of wildflowers overlooking Middletown and enjoyed the peace and quiet. Neither one of them seemed ready to shatter the closeness they'd established.

Right when he blinked open his eyes and cleared his throat, Nova was jabbed by Nola's buzzing phone. It was Amber ranting about a snafu she needed assistance resolving.

And just like that, his last chance to settle things before the wedding vanished.

CHAPTER NINE

The big day had arrived.

Two weeks of drama was plenty for Nova. He pitied men who had to endure a year plus of that bullshit before making things official with the girl of their dreams. If it was ever his turn to march down the aisle, he'd beg for something simple. Maybe a destination wedding. A beach, or a mountain retreat with just him, his woman and their closest family and friends.

In reality, Mustang *had* kept things relatively sane. Until today.

Kaige leaned his hip against the bar of the kitchen where girly shit like cosmetics in a zillion different shades of pink were strewn. He couldn't believe the vision in front of him. Mustang Sally was swaddled in a dress fit for a princess. Rose-colored silk hugged her curves up top then dipped in to her waist, which looked tiny, before flaring to a skirt big enough to hide the entire Hot Rods gang beneath, Buster McHightops included.

It had some kind of crumply look to it like someone had wadded up a ball of paper then made a half-assed effort to smooth it out. Flashes of light danced from crystals sewn in the fabric. It was one of the prettiest things he'd ever seen. A work of art in its own right.

Panicked, Sally didn't match the serene flow of soft fabric. She'd called Nova and begged him to bring Nola upstairs to rectify some crisis he couldn't comprehend through her hiccupping sobs. His heart had dropped as he imagined her needing emergency surgery or something equally dire when actually she'd flipped out about her freaking makeup.

Who was this woman?

"You look beautiful, Sal." Kaige didn't have to lie. She really was stunning. While he'd always appreciated her natural features, she'd done a bang-up job highlighting her assets with subtle yet elegant applications of her own brand of flair. Colorful tattoos and her piercings added enough of her usual badassness to make him relatively certain this wasn't some alien replacement of the girl he'd known most of his life.

"But it's got to be *perfect* today." She balled her fists. "I can't get my liner straight because my damn hands are shaking."

"No worries." Nola stepped in, pressing one finger to her plump lips behind Mustang's back, bidding Kaige to bite his tongue. "Let me help. This'll only take a second."

"Thank you." The bride hugged Nola, worrying her lip as she asked, "How are things going outside? Your sister doesn't need you right now, does she?"

"Nola's my guest, not hired help." Kaige felt it necessary to remind the three of them that he and the consultant were here as a couple today. Something about the ceremony and the atmosphere had him feeling oddly possessive. Hopeful.

"Oh, shush. I'd lend a hand if there were any loose ends. But there's no need. My sis is a pro. Besides, she brought in someone far more competent than me to help her wrangle people. Our mom is out there keeping her eye on things too." Nola surprised them both with that news.

"I'd love to meet her." Kaige was curious about Nola's family. He'd bumped into Amber earlier. The woman had sized him up pretty good with a laser-beam glare before nodding and extending her hand for a firm shake.

How much had Nola shared about the past two weeks?

"Oh, you will." She laughed, flashing her straight, white teeth. "Pretty sure my mom's not going to be able to resist asking you twenty questions before the day is done. Hope you don't mind."

"Nope, I don't." He grinned. "Might as well be introduced the only time I'm wearing something halfway decent. Make a good impression, I hope."

Why was his stomach suddenly doing flip-flops? Charming a woman—or her mother—had never been very difficult for him.

Sally had her head cocked, staring at the two of them. What did she see?

Kaige glanced away.

"So...yeah..." Nola picked up their earlier conversation in an attempt to reassure Sally. "Everything's set and ready. The flowers look unbelievable, the tent is pitched with the extra rain flaps you ordered tied up—doesn't look like you'll need them, it's sunny with blue sky and fluffy white clouds—the caterers are in full swing and your out-of-town guests are already settled in the front rows, heckling your grooms."

"I bet they look so handsome." Mustang blinked rapidly.

"Of course." Nola beamed. "You're one lucky bitch. Now don't go messing up my hard work here. You can cry later, though I'm positive you'll have no reason for sad tears. Want me to put some touch-up supplies in my purse in case you need them down there?"

"Would you mind?" Sally peeked up at Nola with enormous eyes. Kaige could have kissed their miracle worker. "That would be amazing. You did a great job. Sorry I kind of lost it there for a second."

"No problem." Nola tucked the cosmetics in her beaded clutch. "It's an important day. I get that. All I did was draw a teensy hot pink, glittery line. Kaige was right, you're beautiful on your own. Seriously, you look dazzling."

"You both do." Kaige cleared his throat as he approached, the threat of a thermonuclear meltdown seemingly avoided. His gaze raked Nola from her ample cleavage, tucked behind the beaded fringe of her cappuccino-colored dress, to the spikes of her sophisticated yet sexy-as-sin shoes.

He held out his arms and hugged each woman to his chest. How could he care for them both? Want them both? Finally he was understanding how Eli and Al felt about the gang.

Kaige craved Nola. In his bed—son of a bitch, that would be amazing—but also out of it, for the woman she was. A perfect complement to him. Still, he wanted to indulge in the bond with the Hot Rods. Different yet necessary for him to be complete. Hell, he even thought about sharing Nola with the gang. Watching the rest of the guys pleasure her more than any single man was capable of would please him too. He wanted to give her everything good and enjoyable in the world. As much of it as she could handle.

Shit. He was screwed. Because he didn't even know how to ask Nola to consider something like that. Would she assume she was lacking? Or that he didn't value her enough to be selfish and keep her to himself? Would she leave him before they'd really gotten started?

He couldn't handle that possibility.

The door cracked open and Tom's voice called out. "Everyone decent in here? I'm comin' in."

Kaige's heart spasmed when their dad popped inside. The man's eyes bugged out then misted over when he caught sight of Sally. He cleared his throat and turned around for the space of a few heartbeats.

Nola rubbed Kaige's shoulder, helping him relax the knots forming there with each barrage of emotional intensity, which hit him harder than the last. And they hadn't even started the damn wedding yet.

"Good afternoon, Tom." Nola bridged the gap for them, preventing the situation from becoming awkward. She was good at that. At easing friction and keeping things under control.

Kaige wished he had half her social skills.

"Hey, kids." Tom smiled softly as he joined them, clasping one of Sally's hands in his. "You're going to make them so happy. You already do. But...wow."

A speechless Tom was something to see.

"I love you, *Dad*." Mustang hugged him, laying her head on his shoulder. "Thank you."

"Same goes." He moved as if to ruffle her hair then thought better of it when he took in the intricate knot her mane was woven into. "So...I wanted you to have this."

Sally leaned away enough to see what he referred to.

Tom held out a worn velvet bag. "You don't have to put them on if they don't match or whatever, but..."

"Tom, are you kidding?" Mustang's lip quivered. "These are Eli's mom's pearls, aren't they?"

"Uh, yeah." He sniffled.

"I can't accept these." Her shoulders shook as she petted the soft material in her palm.

"She would love for you to have them. To enjoy them. I've seen you admire them, running your finger over them in her jewelry box." He chuckled. "They're pink, even. Trust me. If she were still with us, she'd be setting the clasp around your neck herself today."

Kaige laid his hand on Mustang's trembling back. "I believe he's right, Sally. It's an honor."

"Of course." She nodded vigorously. "I would be proud to wear them."

"Good." Without wasting another second, Tom spun her around and fumbled with the catch.

"Here. Let me." Nola came to the rescue again. She deftly unclipped the gold and realigned it over the nape of Sally's neck. She handed it off to Tom so he could finish the job with minimal fuss.

When Sally rotated slowly to face them once more, the effect had them catching their breath. Perfect. No detail had been left undone. She couldn't get any more spectacular than she was right then.

Before they deteriorated into a sob fest, another knock resounded followed by peals of laughter that could only belong to one gaggle of women. Sure enough, Devon popped her head through the door momentarily before rushing Sally with a high-pitched squee.

Kayla, Morgan and Kate—wives of the infamous Powertools crew—were hot on her heels. Estrogen powerful enough to wither Nova's chest hair flooded the space. Tom was peppered with so many kisses that rings of lipstick dotted his cheeks.

Kaige held Nola's hand and waited for the crew girls to notice their connection. Considering the videochats they'd had lately, it didn't take long for them to put two and two together.

"You must be Nola Brown." Morgan reached out to greet Nola. She didn't settle for shaking hands. Instead she went straight in for a hug. "You're even prettier than Nova said you were."

Kaige did everything possible to keep from blushing. When the hell had he ever been embarrassed around a woman? Damn the crew and their ladies.

Nola beamed. "Thank you."

Did she not realize how attracted he was to her? He could fix that.

The women began to introduce each other and chat ninety miles a minute. Kaige thought he might get whiplash from zigzagging his gaze between the bunch. Thankfully, they gave him an excuse to rejoin his brothers where back slapping and belching would be welcome instead of this insanity.

"Nova, the bossman is looking for you. They want to take some pictures of the guys together." Kate nodded toward the door. "We'll take it from here with Sally. Nola's sister showed us the signal to start her walk down the aisle."

Sally inhaled sharply.

"You're going to do great," Nola reassured her. "I guess I'll go find a seat and see you all down there."

Kaige moved toward the door and Nola shuffled along behind him as if unsure of where she belonged. The women would have none of that.

"Stay, please." Sally bridged the gap and welcomed Nola into their throng. "I'd love to count you with my friends."

Grateful, Kaige touched his finger to his forehead in a salute. "I'll see you ladies in a little while. Knock 'em dead, Sally."

At the last second, he couldn't resist. He pivoted on his heel and returned long enough to swoop down and steal a kiss from Nola, who'd already engrossed herself in conversation with Kayla and Devon. He bent her over his arm to really make an impression on her with his roving mouth.

Someone whistled. It might have been Tom.

Nola sighed as she went limp in his arms, allowing him to do as he pleased. Well, kind of. If he'd had his choice, he'd have shoved her onto the kitchen counter and ruined her outfit, tearing it off of her. Impressed with his own restraint, he placed a light kiss on the corner of her mouth then set her upright before swaggering out the door, pretty pleased with himself.

Tonight was going to be one of the best of his life. Certain, he jogged down the stairs to meet the rest of the misfit mechanics and their crew cousins, who waved at him from Tom's garden.

"I see what was taking so damn long." Holden met him partway across the grass, which looked greener than usual today. Swinger dusted some blush or some other girlie goop off Nova's shoulder then straightened the lapels on his suit. "No one said you had time to sneak a quickie."

"Actually, we didn't even take our clothes off." Electricity hummed through him and he wished they had.

"Hey, that can be the best kind." Mike, the crew's foreman, slapped him on the back. "Way to go, Super Nova."

The rest of the guys huddled around. Though they weren't asking him to kiss and tell, literally, Kaige felt the need to explain. "I meant that it was just a kiss. Except not *just*. You know?"

"Uh-huh," Alanso practically purred. He grasped Eli's hand. From the faraway daze in their eyes, they probably did understand.

"All right, we need to keep on schedule." Amber accompanied the photographer, waving the guys into some semblance of order. "You can give each other shit later. For now, picture time. And if you hurt my sister, I'll kill you. Or at least make you look hideous in this album."

Kaige grinned at her and drew an X over his heart. "I promise. I'm not planning to do anything except make us both very happy."

"I believe that." She smiled. "But for the record…"

"Loud and clear." He nodded. The focus shifted to Alanso and Eli, the day and well-deserved bliss. Surrounded by friends, Kaige grew more optimistic by the second. He had one a-*fucking*-mazing life. And a chance to make it even better.

He wanted the goofy grin on Eli's face for himself. For the first time, he felt like that could be in reach. If only he didn't fuck it up. Could Nola handle the Hot Rods? What about the twisted parts of him like his unusual proclivities and his nasty temper?

Kaige swore to himself then and there that he'd be different from his father. He'd never let anger limit his possibilities. He was done with blaming genetics for his lack of coping. From now on, he'd do better. Be better. For Nola. The guys. Himself.

Repeating the mantra over and over, he couldn't believe the following few hours passed in a blur. Before long he found himself by the pond in Tom's garden. Eli and Alanso stood near the memorials for their mothers as Tom walked Sally down the cobblestone path.

Nova, Holden and Bryce lined up on one side of the trio of honor while Carver, Barracuda and Eli's cousin Joe—representing the crew—flanked them. An intimate gathering of friends, key clients, neighbors and Tom's buddies cheered as they formalized a bond that had existed forever.

Even Buster McHightops—who escaped his crate and dashed into the ceremony with a wildflower stuck under his collar from where he'd tore through the beds—refused to abandon his new owners. Odd as it was, their family kept growing...bigger *and* closer.

Kaige glanced up, his stare meeting Nola's. They smiled at each other. He wondered what it would be like to make the same promises to her one day. Could she be as accepting of their unconventional ways?

So far she hadn't shied away once.

Nova promised himself they'd discuss it tonight. Maybe while snuggled in bed after some terrific sex. He hoped. The need to be intimate with her, not only physically, nearly brought him to his knees in the midst of the supercharged commitment ceremony.

In his heart he pledged himself again to his garagemates. And maybe to the woman watching him as intently as an eagle.

Bryce nudged him with his hulking elbow despite the ceremony going on around them. "You next, huh? Remember, this guy doesn't do tuxes. How about you go really informal? I'd appreciate that."

"Settle down," Holden hissed. "Hang in a few more minutes and we'll get you a glass of wine or three. Soon you won't care that you're dressed up."

"Forget the fancy shit. I'll take a beer." Bryce laughed as Sally subtly gave him the finger behind her back.

Kaige couldn't help but join in. And a few minutes later they were downing a couple cold ones as the reception shifted into gear, a welcome relief even in the fading sun of the late afternoon. Food, great company and plenty more drinks loosened Nova enough to dance with Nola when the music kicked up after dinner.

"Your sister did an amazing job." He leaned in so she could hear his compliment, and hell, just to smell her tantalizing hint of peach. "This is a great party. I'm glad you agreed to share it with me."

She reached up, surprising him with a firm grip on his dreads as she guided his mouth to hers for a taste of heat and chocolate wedding cake. "Me too. My family thinks you're great, by the way. Amber and my mom might already be getting ideas. I'm sorry if they're overbearing."

"Nah." He genuinely liked the women, who obviously had Nola's best interests at heart. "They're terrific. Hell, I think Tom and your mom might be besties. They've been over in that corner talking while they watch the crew's babies for the past two hours."

"Have they?" Nola stood on tippy-toes to peek over his shoulder. "Holy crap. I haven't seen my mom say more than a few sentences to a man socially since..."

A cloud came over her pretty face.

"What?" Nova steered them out of the tent and into the garden. With the ballad at a more manageable level, he sat on the stone bench and pulled Nola into his lap so she didn't get her dress dirty.

"She and Tom aren't so different, I guess." She didn't resist the magnetism between them. She curled into his chest and let him protect her with the banding of his arms. At least as best he could against the unfairness of the universe. "My dad died in a car wreck when I was six. She never got to say goodbye.

None of us did. My mom believed he was run off the road by guys who didn't exactly approve of a white man marrying a black woman. I can't imagine someone caring that much about who you love or how you love. Still, she always assumed it was her fault. For a while she…fell apart, left Amber and I to fend for ourselves and her."

"I'm sorry, Nola." He rubbed his chin over the crown of her head, wondering how far her acceptance could stretch. "That had to be hard."

"Of course. But who of you—" she drew a heart around the Hot Rods tattoo on his neck, "—didn't suffer the same? Hanging out with you guys these past two weeks has opened my eyes. So many people have lived through loss. Learned to move forward however they could. I want to be like you. Not stuck, like my mom was for so long. Maybe still is."

Kaige squeezed her tight. "Everyone handles things in their own way. Hell, if it hadn't been for Tom, I think most of us would have fallen apart. And I suppose, without us, he might have done the same. We got lucky, that's all. Maybe it'd be good for your mom to spend more time with him."

As long as it didn't turn out to be bad for the lonely man. Gloomy memories still haunted him sometimes. Though usually not for long. He was always quick to remind them that he'd had the best gift in the world, and that an entire lifetime of his wife's love wouldn't have satisfied him completely. He considered himself blessed to have had a taste of heaven.

They sat in heavy silence for a while, neither of them feeling the need to speak. It was only when Kaige noticed the goose bumps on Nola's arms that he realized it had been longer than he thought that they cuddled together in solitude.

"Nola…"

"Yeah?" She walked her fingers up his spine to toy with his dreads.

"I think the guests are leaving." When had it gotten so dark out? Stars twinkled above them as crickets and frogs took the place of the DJ's songs. "Want to get out of here too? With me?"

"Where will we go?" She shrugged. "I live with my sister and I have a feeling your apartment is going to be a party pad with the crew in town. I'm kind of in the mood for something…quieter."

"I've always wanted to stay at the fancy hotel on Route 33." He took a shot. "Why don't we see if they have any vacancies?"

She lifted her chin, smiling at him until he accepted her invitation. He guided her lips to his for a warming kiss. They stared into each other's eyes as they exchanged long, gliding passes of their mouths over each other.

"Good idea, Nova," she whispered breathlessly.

"I'll even let you drive my car there if you want." He didn't know where the offer came from. For the first time, the possibility of a non-Hot Rod behind the wheel of his Nova didn't freak him the fuck out. He pulled his keys from his back pocket as he stood, steadying her on those wicked heels, and dangled them in front of her.

She snatched them from his grip. "Hell yeah!"

And like that she was trotting to the tent. The crew guys were in the process of untying the rain flaps, dense canvas that blocked the openings of the pavilion and covered the garden views with opaque fabric. They must be packing up for the night, making things as secure as possible until cleanup began in the morning.

Nola's mother and her sister had already departed along with the rest of the party. He suspected they'd left around the time Tom disappeared into his house to put Abby and Nathan to bed. He'd gladly assumed honorary grandfather duties to let the crew enjoy their rare time in Middletown.

Only the new trio, the crew and the Hot Rods remained, milling about the space. Tables were being folded and stacked in the corners. A surprisingly plush rug remained, taking up the bulk of the tent where the dance floor had been less than an hour ago. Maybe it had been beneath the polished wood to pad the surface.

"Can I talk to you for a second?" Eli approached, cutting between Kaige and Nola.

Nola loosened her grip, allowing their fingers to unmesh. "I want to say goodbye to Sally. Go ahead, I'll be over here."

Nova nodded, hating not having her by his side. "What it is, Cobra?"

"What are your plans for tonight?" The garage owner didn't answer exactly.

"I'm taking Nola somewhere private." The statement rang between them.

"Are you sure that's what you want?" Eli swallowed hard. "Look, we didn't say anything because we didn't want to fuck with your head or make you think we were trying to get you to choose sides, but you have a right to know... Alanso, Sally and I have decided to share our day with the Hot Rods. And the crew. This polyamorous lifestyle we've chosen is about more than just the three of us."

"What?" Kaige took another look at the rearranging going on. The guys weren't simply putting stuff away. They were bringing extra goodies out from beneath a sheet. Soft beanbags, thick mats and something that looked like a glorified hammock now hung in one corner. Extra candles. Holy fucking shit.

They were turning the tent into something out of Arabian nights.

A pleasure palace.

"Yeah." Eli put his hand on Kaige's shoulder. "You know you're welcome here, Nova. And so is Nola. Sally insisted I tell you that. You're part of us and so is anyone you love."

"*Love?*" Kaige swallowed hard. Things were happening too fast. He needed to put on the brakes, but he couldn't. Dangerous curves zoomed at him from every direction and he felt like he was barely keeping himself on the road.

"I wasted a lot of time denying something I knew was true because I was afraid to believe my gut had it right." Cobra was as serious as Kaige had ever seen the guy. "Don't fuck up like I did. Stay. Ask your girl to hang around too. You don't have to be in the thick of it. Sharing yourself or Nola. That's a lot to ask. Something to work up to. No one will say a word if you're doing your own thing on the outskirts. But you'll be here. With us. And that will be enough for now. I don't want you to leave. It won't feel complete without you, Nova."

Kaige didn't know what to say. His mouth had gone dry. He met Nola's gaze from across the room. It practically singed him. How could he navigate around these potholes and keep everyone happy?

"I'll understand if you have to go." Eli sighed. "Though I wish it didn't have to be that way. We're with you whatever you decide. Always. It doesn't have to be a forever choice either. If you leave but you're ready later, cool. If you stay and decide it's not right for you two, fine."

For the second time that night, someone touched Nova's Hot Rods tattoo. Frozen, he looked between Eli and Nola—who had begun her trek back to him from across the tent—as the ink nearly scorched his carotid artery, heated by Eli's hand.

"I think I've got to take things slow and not try to jump from first gear to fifth, you know?" Kaige despised each word. It seemed as if someone put his insides through a rusty engine and pummeled him with the pistons. "I can't scare her off."

Eli didn't speak. Instead he held out his curled fingers, waiting for Kaige to mirror him in a fist bump. "Thanks for being part of the best day of my life. We won't forget about you, even when you're gone. I promise. Come home when you can. With Nola, if she'll ride shotgun with you."

"I have a feeling she's the one in the driver's seat." Kaige laughed.

As if she could hear them, she jingled his keys.

"Are those yours?" Eli's eyes grew wide.

"Yep."

"Well. I guess you're serious, then." Eli grinned.

One more time, they clapped each other on the back before he took a step toward Nola then another. Part of him howled inside even as another portion cheered. He might have grasped her hand too tight, but he couldn't bear loosening his grip as they waved to his friends—who now huddled around the center of the tent, waiting for the chance to get the real party started—then ducked beneath the canvas.

Outside. On their own.

Kaige tried to suck in a deep breath and then another. By the time they reached his car, he thought his guts had been shredded. He hoped he wouldn't bleed to death before Nola could make him forget about everything he'd sacrificed to spend the night with her.

He felt like shit for not appreciating her as much as he should.

And for leaving his gang behind.

Stuck. He spun his wheels.

"Oh, crap." Nola drew his attention as she darted toward the tent. "I forgot my purse. Be right back."

"Wait!" He tried to stop her, but she'd caught him flat-footed. Or maybe some sick part of him wondered what Nola would do if she discovered their secret.

Would she be horrified? Or horny?

Hell, it was too big of a risk to take. What was he thinking?

Kaige sprinted for the pavilion, passing her at the last second. He shouted as he ducked beneath the thick material, "I got it. Go back to the car."

On the other side of the canvas, a whole new world awaited. Half-naked already, a bare-chested Eli smiled. "Changed your mind? Where's Nola?"

"She left her purse. Hurry. Toss it to me." Kaige pointed to where her clutch sparkled from the bar area. He glanced over his shoulder then back, wishing he could snag it and run. Someone had probably moved it from their table when the crew and Hot Rods had worked together to put away the seating more efficiently than the team of set up people had managed.

"Kaige?" Nola was almost right behind him.

Too late, he tried to block her view and usher her out again.

"Stop. What's going on?" Nola's almond eyes grew humongous. "Are you guys…? Wait. I thought it was just Eli, Alanso and Sally who…"

Kaige's heart slammed in his chest as if he'd mashed the pedal to the metal on a supercharged ride. He couldn't find the words to explain.

So Sally did it for him. "Nola, there are some things you don't know about us yet. But we'd love to show you. We're more than friends. All of us. Kaige included. Watch. It's simpler than talking it out. Easier to understand when you see for yourself."

"My *wife* is right. Why don't you stay, *chica*?" Alanso extended an invitation in his seductive accent. "Make Nova a lucky guy, would you? Share tonight with us."

"I swear, Nola, I didn't know this was going down. Not really. Not until a few minutes ago." Kaige turned toward her as he wiped his free hand over his mouth. Was he drooling? Maybe a little. Torn, he didn't know if he should run forward and join the throng or grab Nola and race to his car before temptation stole her from him. He wanted to promise that they could walk away and that she would be enough. He couldn't force himself to lie when he didn't know if it was the truth.

He didn't want to hurt her.

He didn't want to hurt the Hot Rods.

He didn't want to hurt himself.

The odds of managing all three of those things seemed about as likely as him ever working on an Alfa Romeo Carabo.

How the hell was he going to fix this?

CHAPTER TEN

Nola blinked to clear her mind of the abundance of gorgeous of men, who ranged from fully clothed to naked and every stage in between, spread like a feast on the plush rug. She could hardly believe that the women they loved were so...indulged.

And yet she could.

Hadn't she seen the evidence of the Hot Rods' relationship day after day in the shop? Hadn't she known, on some level, that they were more than friends? Easy touches, intimacy that extended beyond best pals or even siblings...she'd seen it, but hadn't allowed herself to recognize it for what it truly was.

If she had, the revelation would have crushed the burgeoning hope that she and Nova had a special connection. How could what they nurtured compare to that?

A pang of regret and loss nearly had her doubling over with cramps.

Because she knew there was no way she could let Kaige turn his back on his gang, even if he'd been willing to walk away. For her.

Nothing he was saying could have shown her more how much he cared about her, desired her, than that had. Unfortunately, that meant she had to repay him in kind. And let him go. Otherwise, when the chrome of this new link they'd formed dulled, he'd regret it. Maybe even resent her for taking him from his friends.

Her heart cracked as the fairytale ending to their whirlwind affair evaporated. She couldn't picture Kaige happy if he lost the Hot Rods.

Nola took a huge breath, hoping to reverse the crushing pressure on her chest. Then she looked into the gleaming blue eyes of the best man she'd ever *almost* had.

"It's okay if you've changed your mind. About the hotel." She smiled a bit as she reached up to kiss him gently. "You should be with them, not me."

He didn't deny that he craved joining with the people surrounding them. Instead, he considered so long his neck was in jeopardy of wearing out as he looked at her, then the action already heating up beneath the tent, then back to her again.

Over and over.

Nola let him think it through. She would support him, show him that she understood, that he was a deserving man, even if things didn't work out between them.

Damn it, she cared for him. A lot.

"What if I want both?" He squeezed her hands as if afraid to let go.

The urgency in his gaze caused her heart to skip a few beats. Participating in an orgy had never been on her bucket list. But when she thought about the guys that had surrounded her for the past two weeks, she couldn't deny their appeal.

Would it be worse to have joint custody of Kaige than to lose him? Better, could she enjoy their decadent proposition instead of tolerating it for her partner's sake?

As she watched Eli and Alanso flank Sally, she couldn't deny her fascination.

What would it be like if Kaige were so generous? If he let Bryce or Holden or any of his friends do the same for her?

She shivered.

"Am I really invited to this after party?" She surprised the hell out herself—and Kaige too, judging by his slack jaw, when she double-checked with Eli.

"Absolutely," Sally answered for everyone.

The rest of the Hot Rods nodded furiously. The Powertools crew stood guard around them, as if protecting their distant friends from whatever might happen next. Kaige took her hand and laid it over his heart so she could feel the beat there kick into overdrive, pounding so hard a faint echo of the drumming showed in his throat.

"I'm sorry I can't give you only myself. That this is something I need right now. I never meant to deceive you." Nova tried to make her understand his compulsion. "It's kind of a new thing for us. Though it's not like we haven't always been close. It's another way. Another tie. You shouldn't have to sacrifice traditional expectations because I'm a freak by nature. I can't explain good enough—"

"Hey, stop." She covered his mouth. "Quit apologizing for who you are. I happen to really l—*like* the man you're making excuses for. Quirks and all."

"Seriously?" As if afraid to believe, he swallowed hard.

"Hell yeah." Nola leaned forward to whisper in his ear, divulging a secret. "You and your friends are so smokin', I've been having trouble sleeping through the night without waking up in a sweaty mess from the naughty dreams you've inspired. Maybe I've wondered what it would be like...with more than one of you... You know, Sally's been putting impure thoughts in my mind with how freaking happy she is. Now I guess I really know why."

Kaige trapped her close, nipping her neck slightly below her ear. To mark her so she knew he was serious, or so the other guys saw he had claimed her, she wasn't sure.

"Would you like me to make those fantasies come true?" He growled. "Because I am so up for that, it's not funny."

Nola wriggled her hips against the hard-on that had materialized the moment he realized exactly how his friends intended to spend their honeymoon. She hadn't been able to help herself from peeking, and remember how well he'd filled her.

"No kidding." She slid her hand to the front of his trousers and cupped him.

"But I need you to understand that you're mine first, and vice versa. Anything they do to you is as if I'm doing it through them. Does that make sense? Shit, I know it doesn't. But..."

"Kaige, if you don't zip your lips and take this dress off me soon to start making good on all this talk, I can't be responsible for what happens next." Her voice took on a husky rasp she was sure she'd never heard from herself before.

No surprise, he seemed to find it even more alluring than usual.

Nova scooped her into his arms and trotted across the space separating them from the rest of the gang. In the center of the tent, the six guys and the woman she considered an extension of her new boyfriend welcomed them with open arms.

Ties slithered to the floor along with belts. Highly polished dress shoes clunked into the corners of the tent. The three couples and one trio of the crew, some of them already naked, each occupied a corner of the floor. The rest divested themselves of their formal trappings even faster than the Hot Rods, if that was possible.

Nola whimpered when Kaige set her in the center of those special guests, men and women she now realized must be role models for their Hot Rod protégés. Carver along with Nova knelt at her feet, slipping her pumps from them one by one.

Afraid of losing her balance in the whirlwind of insanity and ecstasy whipping up around her, she must have whimpered.

"It's all right, Nola. I've got you. Meep's part of me, remember?" Kaige schooled her.

"Yeah. Yes. I do." She blinked rapidly, as if trying to clear haze from her lust-soaked mind. "It's...a lot, though. God. Overwhelming. In a good way."

This time she shivered, and not from any kind of chill when it was at least a million degrees in their steamy oasis. She couldn't help but stare at Alanso and Eli. The partners unwrapped Sally from infinite layers of silk—dress, petticoats, corset and garters. Roman, Holden and Bryce helped out by unlacing various obstacles, swiping the stockings from her legs and tearing a pair of lace panties from her ass before spanking her tight rear.

When the sight overloaded her senses, Nola briefly shut her eyes, trying to take a visual break before her circuits fried. Instead, her gaze landed on Mike, who had placed his nude wife in one of the hammocks they'd erected. Already, he'd buried his head between her thighs, eating her with a gusto he hadn't even reserved for the gourmet banquet they'd been served earlier.

Around them, sights and sounds of pleasure abounded. It was a gluttony of passion.

Privileged to be in the midst of such a superpower, a lot like dancing in the center of a tornado funnel, Nola drew from the energy arcing from couple to couple, man to man, and woman to woman. Kaige did too, if his growing grin, wolfish and sexy, had anything to say about it.

Why the hell hadn't he clued her in to this sooner?

Honestly, if he had, she might have run from such entanglements.

Now the stakes were too high to fold.

"Tell me if it's too much," Kaige murmured as he tucked her hair behind her ear. "We can back off or even leave if you're uncomfortable."

"I will. But I don't think that's going to happen." Nola smiled at him, trying to stay open-minded. It'd been a fundamental tenant of how she was raised. Her mother had hammered home the value of acceptance and the consequences of being ignorant. "Why don't you worry about having a damn good time?"

"I already am." He kissed her again and again, until they got lost in the moment. When she opened her eyes, things were progressing rapidly.

Nola gawked at his six male partners. Their cocks stood at full attention, ready to give their companions the most valuable gift of the occasion. Themselves. And their unconditional love.

In the background, Neil perched on a stool while Devon and James tag-teamed him in a tandem blowjob. To one side, Kayla crooked a finger at Dave. The guy's hard-on caused even Nova's eyes to bulge. Proportional to his gigantic frame, he was hung like a horse. Morgan had Joe laid out on his back while she lowered herself onto his shaft. She rode her husband with a sensual fluidity that Nola envied.

Could she be such a temptress for Kaige?

It was a lot to process. Sure, she'd imagined Sally, Eli and Alanso playing together, entwining their desires. But this... This was something new altogether.

Disgust or fear never entered her mind.

Hedonistic freedom raced through her veins.

She'd never felt so in control of her destiny.

Or as fortunate. Kaige had such wonderful people so completely ingrained in his life. A safety net he could trust implicitly. And now they were extending that same support to her, through him.

She beamed up at Kaige.

His shoulders widened and his fingers uncurled. For the first time, she saw the man without the baggage he normally lugged around. What a difference.

"I don't think I've seen you relax completely." Nola purred as she ran her fingers over his body, divesting him of his jacket, then working on the row of buttons down his crisp white shirt. The feel of him hard and waiting beneath his clothes drove her mad.

"I wouldn't exactly say I am yet." He winked. "But I might be when we're finished here."

"Mmm." Nola tugged his shirt from his trousers and flung it to the growing pile of garments. Carver sidled up next to them, with Roman standing behind him, his hands on Meep's shoulders as the smaller guy sank to his knees.

"Come on, slow poke." Barracuda kept them on task.

Next thing Nola knew, Carver had unbuckled Kaige's belt and relieved him of his pants. Nova shrugged. Efficiency he seemed to appreciate if it meant he was that much closer to fusing them.

She wasn't going to complain.

Maybe it would be for good this time.

"I can't believe you're seeing all of me and you're still looking at me like...*that*," he murmured.

"I've seen you naked before, big guy." She patted his chest. "Nothing to complain about."

He laughed then waved at his nude skin, decorated so brilliantly. "Thanks, but I'm talking about more than this."

His heart and soul were laid bare for her judgment.

"I think you're amazing," she promised.

"Same goes." He crushed her in a hug. "A million times over."

Nola smiled. She stared at Kaige as she lifted her arms and allowed Roman to peel off her dress. Standing before him in a white strapless bra and matching panties, she seemed to have his full attention.

"I wish I could paint, like Mustang." He sighed.

She could say the same. She'd never get tired of looking at him. Especially not with that twinkle in his eye that proclaimed his daredevil side was ready to be unleashed for one hell of a romp.

When Roman raised her hand, kissed her knuckles then spun her in a slow-motion pirouette, Nola realized they were checking out the view from behind. He grabbed her full ass and spread her cheeks a bit, enough to make her g-string ineffective in blocking even a sliver of her bottom.

Carver kneeled to lay a kiss on each of her cheeks. "You're damn fine, Nola."

"Thanks." She swallowed when Roman and Kaige each took one of her hands and lowered her to the carpet beneath them. Bryce joined them, leaving Holden to help Alanso prep Eli to take him in his ass while Eli fucked their wife.

It seemed like it might be one of their favorite ways to chain mate. It certainly was hot to watch.

Swinger would likely get his cock sucked by either Alanso or Sally, whichever had more sense about them at the moment. In the background, the Powertools crew cheered them on while helping their partners enjoy the show as much as they did, providing eye candy for the Hot Rods while they were at it.

Kayla called out to Sally, "You know, some day when you're ready for advanced tricks, you might want to try fooling around with Nola. A woman is best for finding her way around another woman's body."

Mustang froze, as did Nola. Then she squeaked, "Seriously? Do you guys...girls, I mean..."

"Yep." Devon beamed. "Variety is the spice of life, you know. At least for me. But it took a while to work up to it. It's not for everyone either. Morgan's not really into girl-on-girl stuff."

"And that's okay," Mike explained. "You'll figure out what each other's boundaries are and how you fit together in infinite combinations. It'll take time. No reason to rush. Enjoy each new pleasure as it comes."

"Literally," Neil joked. "And comes and comes…"

James smacked his partner on his washboard abs, causing not one iota of damage.

Kaige watched Nola as if hunting for some sign of repulsion, which he wouldn't find. It was obviously a departure from what she'd considered to be her sexual orientation. After tonight, though, who knew where she'd stand?

"Would you like that, Kaige?" She couldn't resist teasing. "To see me kiss another woman?"

His cock leaked at the thought alone, though she knew he'd never pressure her. She and Sally scooted closer to each other, by some tacit understanding, allowing the men doting on them both to stay more connected too.

Nola felt empowered by their acceptance, unafraid of putting herself on display or of appreciating the muscled forms of men—and women—who worked hard for a living.

Kaige growled, then charged as if he couldn't wait another instant.

He settled on top of her, his cock riding the furrow of her slit. Within seconds, he was coated in her arousal. A slight tilt of his hips and he'd notched the tip of his cock inside her.

"I missed you," she murmured. "Let's not wait to do this again."

"Your best proposal yet." He groaned as her heat must have set him ablaze. He rocked slightly, locking their bodies as his head popped inside the ring of muscles guarding her opening.

And with that, the rest of the Hot Rods began to deepen their own embraces. Sally soon found herself full of Eli as he welcomed Alanso. Holden slipped between Mustang's and Al's mouths, satisfied with either person suckling him. Bryce pivoted, alternating toying with Nola and Sally.

Kaige advanced farther into Nola's body. He buried himself balls deep before kissing her thoroughly while they both overcame the initial shock of that intense binding.

Sally declared her love and devotion to her husbands then the rest of the group.

The Powertools crew echoed her sentiments to their mates and each other.

Overcome by the positive energy surrounding them, Nola urged Kaige to move.

She smiled into his eyes, trailing her fingers over his lips then his dreads and on to his tattoos. Exchanging such tenderness with one special person, as well as a group of close friends, amplified the intensity of their intimate joining.

"I'm proud to show you off." He grunted as he buried himself in her. "You make me feel so good. They can tell, Nola. I'm content. For the first time. Because of you."

As Kaige made love to her—slow and gentle, finally—his friends got in on the action. Bryce and Carver ducked close to each take one of her breasts into their mouths. They suckled even as their hands wandered down her torso, and Nova's.

The sensations they added to the already incredible fucking Kaige gave her pushed Nola higher than she'd ever gone before. They kept up their manipulations, worming their fingers between the writhing bodies of their friends to toy with her clit or Nova's balls on occasion.

Kneeling, bent at the waist, Carver flashed his ass at Roman and took a quick break from suckling her to ask, "Aren't you going to fill me up, Barracuda?"

"I thought—" The oldest member of the Hot Rods cleared his throat. "Maybe, just for tonight. This one time..."

Even Kaige paused as Roman spit out his shocking offer. "I thought you might like to show me what all the fuss is about."

Carver spun to face his roommate. "Are you saying...?"

"Yeah. If that's something you're interested—"

He never did finish that thought. Because Meep's mouth crashed down on Roman's. They wrestled each other with a ferocity that had Nola begging Kaige to resume his steady fucking in order to replace some of the tension with delicious friction.

Nola sighed and moaned. "They're so hot together. Fuck me harder, Kaige."

He didn't have much choice. The sight of Roman surrendering to Carver had to get to him too.

Though soon enough, Meep ended their kiss and dropped to his back beside Nola. They left only enough room for Roman to straddle the guy. Carver said, "You should run the show. You can decide how deep to take me and how fast that way. Plus I'll be able to jerk you off."

Nola clenched around Kaige. She cried out, drawing encouragement from the Powertools ringing them.

"Better yet," Dave suggested, "why not let Nola do the honors so you can concentrate on supporting your guy?"

Sounded like a plan to her. What would it be like to touch one man while another fucked her so perfectly? Now that they'd offered the possibility, she had to know.

Before the idea had even flown from the crew member's mouth, Nola had her hand up and curled around Roman. Watching her dark fingers on his lighter skin elicited a groan from Kaige. He grit his teeth.

"Is this okay?" she verified.

"Better than." He panted. "The way you didn't hesitate to please my friend... Damn that's so fucking hot. So is the way your pussy is strangling me."

She did her best to distract Barracuda as he impaled himself on Carver for the first time. His virgin ass had no trouble accepting the modest shaft and soon he was riding his roommate in sync with Kaige, who caressed her from the inside out.

Holden stared in wonder.

"Nova?" he grumbled.

"Yeah," was the best Kaige seemed to be able to manage. Roaring, with his head thrown back, he looked as if he tried to fend off his rising ecstasy.

"I gotta be inside someone. Linked." Swinger's gaze ping-ponged from couple to couple or clump of people to clump of other people where the distinctions began to get hazy. All around, lovers united.

"What's wrong with my mouth?" Carver rose an eyebrow. Dotted with sweat, his forehead declared him incapable of much more than enduring the blazing rapture Roman had inspired with both his tight ass and his trust.

"Or mine?" Nola surprised herself again.

"Generous *and* loving—you hit it big, Nova." Holden slapped Kaige's shoulder.

Thrilled to make her guy proud, she reached out her tongue and licked the underside of Swinger's head. And that was all it took. Within five seconds, she had a mouthful of one Hot Rod and a handful of another to go with the thick shaft filling her pussy. The taste of pure passion sent her to the next level of rapture.

Beside them, Eli roared. "Fuck, that's hot."

As if to prove their point, one of the Powertools loosed a long, low moan that could only mean they were coming. Several others followed suit. Knowing their sharing enhanced people's desire instead of dampening it seemed to reassure the Hot Rods.

Nola could say it did the same for her.

They grew more vocal. More bold. More vigorous in their fucking.

Nola didn't realize wetness trailed from the corners of her eyes until Kaige glanced down at her. He stuttered within her. "Are you okay?"

Holden withdrew from her mouth long enough to let her explain her tears of joy.

"It's so beautiful. So powerful. So much...*more*...than I could have hoped for tonight." She hugged Nova fiercely. "Thank you for including me. For making me a part of something bigger."

Kaige's cock bulged. He angled his hips so that his blunt head, complete with the sexy metal piercing, prodded her right about...*there*.

With a gasp and shriek she hoped were more adorable than slasher-flick, Nola balanced on the brink of orgasm. Holden assisted her demise by toying with her breasts while Kaige repeated his targeted strokes. From next to them, Alanso began to curse a steady stream of Spanish. They were all toeing the line.

Together.

Roman crumbled first. He went stiff on top of Carver, groaning and clutching Kaige's arm to steady himself as he loosed a steady stream of come across his roommate's chest. The smaller man pumped his own release into Roman's ass as Nola continued to stroke the hard-on spurting through her fingers.

The proof of her participation in such a momentous sharing tipped her over the edge. She stared straight into Kaige's eyes as she allowed herself to be swept away. His pupils dilated as she began to come beneath him. Her whole body quaked and still she managed to swallow as Holden joined her in ultimate rapture.

Kaige didn't stand a chance at resisting the rhythmic pulls of her pussy on his cock. He shot inside her over and over, pouring himself deep into her unprotected womb. They'd have to discuss the possible repercussions later, but she found herself unafraid of any outcome.

The idea of creating a new life with Nova, in addition to the one she hoped they'd share after tonight, didn't scare her in the least. *Please let him feel the same way.*

His tantalizing smile, which spread when Holden slipped from her lips, gave her plenty of hope that he did.

Still joined, they watched from front-row seats as Eli, Alanso, Sally and Bryce came to a similar conclusion. Exhausted, sated and replete, the nine of them collapsed into a loose pile of limbs. In a ring around them, the Powertools had done the same, each of them holding hands with their neighbor.

Whispered praise, soft moans and gentle sighs were the only sounds in the tent for some time afterward. Kaige clung tight to Nola, letting her feel the steady thump of his heart, which pressed to her bosom.

Nola broke their silence. "Safe to say I'm not bolting any time soon. You're sure you don't mind sharing the rest of your day, and your guys—longer term—with me, Sally?"

She nibbled her lower lip as she regarded Mustang from the corners of her eyes.

"Honey, there's plenty to go around." The gracious girl didn't hesitate for a moment. "I'm not a superwoman. Entertaining them is hard fucking work."

"You love every minute." Alanso smacked her on her bubble butt. Hopefully the men wouldn't mind someone a hell of a lot more statuesque. They'd be as different as vanilla and chocolate. A flavor for everyone.

"I do." She nuzzled her second husband as she echoed the vow from earlier. "But I'm not so greedy that I don't want to see Nova happy too. Every Hot Rod. They like you, Nola. So do I."

The other woman didn't shy away from meeting Nola's gaze as she granted her seal of approval. And damn if it didn't feel good. "Thank you, Sally. I know what they mean to you. I respect that. And them."

She blushed as she tucked her face against Kaige's chest. He hugged her tight.

"Same goes, sweetheart." Bryce trailed his knuckles down her arm. "What's important to one of us is protected by all. Don't forget that we've got your back."

"And we have yours," Mike piped in. The crew had shuffled closer, surrounding them in another layer of positive energy and friendship. "Just like you were there for us when we needed you. We'll never forget it."

Mike reached out and shook hands with Eli, then Alanso.

"Congratulations on your big day." Kate patted both men on the head before hugging Sally. None of them seemed overly concerned by their nudity, which kind of made sense considering one of their members owned a naturist resort. "It's been a long time coming. You deserve every ounce of happiness I can see they're giving you. And always will."

"I'm so glad you made it out here." Sally grinned. "We'll be up to the apartment in a little bit. Maybe after another round or two."

"I hope you don't mind if we bail. Kate and Morgan are antsy to take the babies off Tom's hands. They should be asleep, but..." Joe nodded to his wife. "The moms haven't exactly mastered this separation thing yet."

"Like you're not eager to tuck Nathan in yourself?" Kayla called him on his bullshit.

"Well, yeah..." He grinned. "Okay I'm as bad as they are, I admit it."

"Worse. You're way more of a mother hen." Neil jabbed his friend in the gut. "Come on, let's go check on the boy. It isn't like we won't see the Hot Rods again since we're camping out in their living room. Good thing your place is enormous!"

The crew filed out, their members each making some personal goodbye. Nola was included in their hugs and waves as much as any other person in the room. She wriggled her fingers and smiled before whispering, "It's amazing. For the first time, I feel like it's not just my family against the world."

"We *are* your family," Kaige told her. "If you'll have me. Them. What do you say?"

"I say, can we do that again? Except this time..." She stared directly into Kaige's eyes. "I want you to watch them ravish me. And I want to see them do the same to you. We're strong enough to feel this even if other people are doing the fucking for us. Right?"

"Shit yes." He groaned. "What do you think about that, Sal?"

"Green light." The other woman had no qualms. "Let's start those engines, boys."

Holden skidded to Kaige's side and started granting Nola's wishes before Nova had actually consented. His delighted gurgle as Swinger's fist surrounded his already re-hardened cock was proof enough that he had no objections.

Nola welcomed Bryce's broad hands on her waist. After all, someone had to hold her upright when Carver began to ply her pussy with his tongue while Roman nudged the saturated opening with the head of his condom-covered cock.

It was going to be a long, exhausting night.
The best of her life, she was sure.
At least until the next one.
And the one after that.
On and on.
And on.

EPILOGUE

Nola froze the swinging of her legs, crossed at the ankles, where they dangled off Eli's desk in the Hot Rods' main office. She clenched her thighs as the seven guys she'd come to crave strutted into the space at once, making it seem to shrink. Last to enter was Sally, though the other woman joined her, hopping up onto the desk and slinging an arm around her shoulders.

It hadn't taken more than a month to feel at home here. So why did this seem like a staff meeting gone wrong, or maybe some kind of disciplinary intervention?

Before she could get too freaked out, Kaige interrupted her worrywart tendencies by kissing her silly. She wrapped her arms around him, wondering if she had it wrong. Maybe their serious expressions had really been lust?

Could they be looking for a midday romp instead of some kind of business?

She'd be down for that.

Nola peeked over Kaige's shoulder when he allowed her room for a breath. The glass door remained unlocked. A customer could waltz in any minute. Never mind Tom.

She respected Eli's dad too much to be caught with her pants down, literally, on the clock.

"Guys?" She addressed them all but looked to Nova to answer her.

"We've got an offer for you, if you're interested," he began.

"Here? Now?" Her stare darted between them before Sally giggled, letting her off the hook.

"Not *that* kind of job. Though I've never known them to turn one down." Mustang patted her shoulder. "What he's saying is that we'd like to hire you. Full time. To work for Hot Rods."

"Yeah, that." Kaige nodded, his dreads mesmerizing her as always. "I hope you know how I feel about you personally. More every day. But on top of that, you're damn good at designing and presenting proposals. I'm not sure I ever did make that clear enough."

"You have." She ran her knuckles along some of his tattoos. "Thank you. But we're nearly done with the strategy briefing. What else would I do?"

"Babe, the way you made it so easy to visualize..." Bryce cut in. "We'd make a killing selling upgrades and style packages to customers if we had you there to make them see what we dream up."

"Seriously?" A lump formed in Nola's throat as an invisible rubber band of tension snapped in her belly. She'd been taking longer than ever on this damn project, knowing that when she finished... Well, it'd never be like this again. Spending all her time with the gang she was coming to adore.

No, *love*.

Even her mom had started popping in for lunches with Nola...or Tom. The two of them had hit it off. Amber and her mother kept asking what the status of Nola's relationship with Kaige was. She didn't know what to label it.

It simply felt right.

And that was good enough for her family.

They wholeheartedly approved of her new circle of friends. Someday she might have to tell them how close they truly were. Because she knew if she accepted this offer, there'd be no going back. She'd be one of them.

Officially.

"God, yes. I'd love to be part of the shop. Of the Hot Rods." She knuckled away a drop of moisture from the corner of her eyes. Amber would understand. Hell, she hadn't needed a partner in Brown & Brown for a while now. She had things under control and might appreciate the chance to take the firm in her own direction.

Carver whooped even as Bryce and Holden slapped each other on the back.

Roman moved toward her, but before he could spit out whatever he was on the brink of sharing, a grime-covered man entered the shop. The reek of cigarettes rolled off him as if he'd chained smoked twelve packs before coming in.

"Who's in charge around here?" the man demanded in a too-loud shout.

Kaige's cheeks grew red at the interruption and the crass greeting of their crasher. Nola laid her hand on his arm and squeezed lightly. Stiffness leached from his muscles and he turned to her with a rueful smile.

His temper dissolved easily when she was there. Learning to read the signs of his escalation had been easy, and together they could usually diffuse him before he lost his cool. Proud of his progress, she hugged him around his waist.

"Can we help you?" Eli asked the intruder.

"Well, it ain't me I'm worried about." The guy wiggled his brows. "Some rich bitch is stranded on the side of Route 33 in a maroon Maserati. She paid me a thousand bucks to find a tow truck for her. Says her phone is dead too."

Bryce stood up so fast he knocked over a rack of custom license plate holders. Ignoring the mess, he asked, "What model?"

"Hell if I know. It's a Maserati, dude. I never seen one before."

"What does this woman look like?" He acted like Buster McHightops with his favorite chew toy. Relentless. Unlike the usually laid-back giant. The rest of the guys watched the exchange with raised brows.

"Tall. Real blonde. Like a movie star. Bright blue eyes..."

With every description, Rebel seemed to clench his jaw harder. Nola worried about his dental work.

"...and perfect tits except for a little mole right about here." The jerk pointed to his left pec.

Bryce put his hands on his knees and sucked in a deep breath.

"If you ain't got anything available, I can go back and fetch her." The guy's small bulge was obvious from where Nola sat. Kaige tucked tighter against her, as if to shield her from the creeper. From his bed in the corner, Buster growled. "I offered to drive her into town, but she turned me down. Guess my truck is too dirty for a broad like that."

Nola didn't think it had anything to do with the state of the guy's ride. The woman had been smart to stay put. They had to go help her. But what the hell was up with Rebel?

Holden put his hand on Bryce's back. He asked quietly, "You okay?"

"No. Not really." His low bass sounded strained. Odd.

"You know that chick?" Alanso wondered.

Eli shooed the informant out, assuring him he'd earned his fee. When the guy was gone, they turned to Rebel. "Who is she?"

"My past," he snarled. "I've got this."

"I'll come with." Carver offered.

"No. I'm going alone." Bryce didn't allow any other discussion on the topic, though Buster refused to stay put. When his adopted master moved toward the storefront, the dog was right on his heels. Rebel stormed out of the office, smashing the door into the garage wall hard enough Nola expected it to have cracked. The giant guy grabbed some keys off the pegboard on the wall, clipped Buster's leash on, then stalked to the lot. The roar of the tow truck's diesel came a few seconds later.

"Well, this should make for an interesting evening." Holden grinned. He reveled in mischief.

"What a welcome, Nola." Sally squeezed Nola's hand. "We'll celebrate later. Promise."

"I thought that's what we've been doing for the past several weeks." Nola assured them it was fine. She had the important things she needed in her life. Starting with the man lingering beside her, where she hoped he'd always stay.

"Good point." Roman nodded. "But like birthday cake, you never can have too much great sex."

"In that case, we'll have a party. Hot Rods style. As soon as we make sure Rebel's okay." She wouldn't turn them down. Not now, or ever.

After scanning each of their smiling faces, she turned to Kaige.

The pure adoration radiating from him warmed her inside and out. She went into his arms easily as he plucked her from the desk. "Eli, I'm taking the afternoon off. I have something I want to do. With Nola. In my car. It'll take a while to get right. Call if you need us. If Rebel does. But otherwise...we'll see you for dinner. Probably."

Nola wrapped her arms around her man's shoulders as he toted her to his ride. She knew they'd finally christen that backseat properly. And she couldn't wait to drive him wild.

After all, she'd taken to calling him Super Nova like his friends. Not because of his temper anymore, but because of the intensity they generated between them when they exploded together.

It seemed fitting.

She hoped to set astrological records tonight...and every other.

For the rest of their lives.

THE ADVENTURES DON'T END
HERE! KEEP READING...

Love is waiting on the wrong side of the tracks.

Bryce Ellington has been keeping a really big bomb of a secret. And the platinum-blonde detonator is wearing five-inch heels, standing next to a broken-down Maserati. His fellow Hot Rods have never pried into the past that forced him from the only life he'd ever known, from the girl he loved. But as recognition dawns in Kaelyn DuChamp's eyes—just before those eyes roll back in a dead faint—he realizes he's going to have a lot of explaining to do. And a ton of damage to control.

When Kaelyn's great escape from her controlling family fizzles—complete with a face-plant in the dirt—she's relieved to see the flash of tow truck lights. Then shocked to recognize the man behind the wheel. The best friend she's been missing for too many years.

Once Kaelyn collapses in Bryce's arms, he never wants to let her go. But if she spills his secret, the resulting scandal could destroy everything he and the Hot Rods have worked for, built, and loved.

Warning: Contains abuse of designer heels, bubble baths gone wild, an inexperienced heroine who can kick some serious ass, smokin' hot sex as many ways as you can imagine it...and some you haven't.

EXCERPT FROM REBEL ON THE RUN, HOT RODS BOOK 4

Flashing amber lights crested the hill, followed by a monstrous tow truck decked out in chrome and metallic onyx paint. Enormous fireball graphics exploded over the hood, as if the vehicle plowed through an inferno. Its driver seemed proportionally huge behind the wheel. Either that or the company had a grizzly bear for a mascot and allowed the thing to respond to emergencies.

Darn. Please don't let this guy be sketchy too, she prayed.

A lifetime of etiquette instruction took control and Kaelyn attempted to groom her disheveled hair, fix her suit, haul her shoe from the muck and school her face into a calm mask of indifference all at once. Illusions were the only source of power she had left.

Instead she only managed to turn in circles, put some color in her cheeks and propel her heart rate from elevated to a ridiculous, extra-nervous thumping that pulsed in her fingertips while she began to perspire.

Kaelyn deflated, admitting to herself that her great escape had more in common with a fledgling tumbling out of a nest than a majestic eagle learning to spread its wings and soar. She stared at the long, broad shadow her unlikely savior cast as he rounded the hood of his behemoth machine. Please, let him be decent.

Did such people exist? She wouldn't bet on it anymore.

The clomp of his boots on the tar and gravel of the road was sure and steady as he ate up the distance between them with the immense length of his strides. Laying her shaky, sweaty palms against her thighs, she forced herself to lift her chin.

Kaelyn prepared to do something she rarely did. Okay, never had done before.

Ask for help.

Beg for charity from a stranger no less. Humbling.

Usually she was the one organizing benefits for those less fortunate.

Except, when she scanned from his leather boots to his ripped jeans, which hugged his tree-trunk thighs, to a grease-stained T-shirt that showcased his impressive chest and broad shoulders, everything she'd rehearsed—about how she'd work off her debt, or leave an IOU behind—stuck in her throat.

Or maybe that lump was her heart.

Heaven knew that worthless thing had stopped cold.

Because her savior seemed awfully familiar. He was what her best friend might have looked like if she'd seen the kid grow into an unapologetically sexy man. Instead, his rebellious teenaged urges had led him to a life roaming Europe as some reclusive rich playboy, who'd forgotten about the girl next door by the time his father's private jet touched down across the pond. She glanced at her inherited Maserati and swallowed around the pain that still lanced her when she indulged in memories of Bryce Ellington IV.

If he hadn't abandoned her, maybe everything could have been different.

Wishful thinking, she knew from endless experience, didn't change what had happened. But it could ease the pain for a moment. She thought of him—drawing on the strength he'd embodied before he'd gone completely selfish—to get her through this, like other rough times.

It must be a sign that this man was Bryce's spitting image. Part of her relaxed.

Unfortunately, she must have whispered his name.

And that's when the world went insane.

"Yeah, Kae. It's me." The grim set of his mouth didn't make him seem happy to see her. "I thought maybe you wouldn't recognize me. It's been so long. And I'm...a hell of a lot different. But, I'm not going to lie. Part of me is glad you haven't forgotten."

It was the twinkle in his steely eyes that proved the impossible things spilling from this not-stranger's wicked mouth. Surely, his rough and rugged exterior had nothing in common with the groomed adolescent she'd known. Still, something unmistakable reached out and grabbed her.

"Bryce?" she croaked again. Louder this time. It felt rusty rolling off her tongue. Confusion had her lids fluttering as she struggled to believe what she saw. Completely overwhelmed, she blinked up at him. Squinted. Scrubbed her eyes.

The vision remained.

This was no rich, idle son. No, he was a blue-collar sex god right here in the US of freaking A. Forget another continent, she'd found him less than two states away. What happened to the stories his father had told her of Bryce's escapades with an endless stream of gorgeous foreign women, with whom she could never compare?

Was nothing she believed the truth?

"Hi." He reached toward her when the periphery of the world turned black, though he paused as if to admire her, unaware of the way things melted into a Dali-scape in her vision. "Damn. You grew up fine, didn't you?"

She might have offered some witty remark if her entire mouth hadn't gone numb along with the rest of her body. It wasn't every day she saw the ghost of BFFs past.

"Crap!" He jogged, closing the gap between them with a couple giant strides, his arms outstretched to brace her.

Kaelyn retreated, afraid to let him touch her. This couldn't be happening.

"But you're gone!" she shrieked as she stumbled backward.

"I'm not. I never really left the country." He winced as she wondered if he could be some kind of imposter. "Who else would know about the times we snuck over to your tree house and camped out, spending the summer nights looking at the stars and telling each other about our dreams? Or the stray cat we made our pet out there? Remember the time you snuck Mr. Whiskers that fancy salmon from your dad's Christmas party?"

"Bryce? Is this some sick trick my father is playing?" Anything made more sense than what this impersonator spouted.

"No, Kae." He swallowed hard. "It's really me."

"I see." She'd never punched a person in her life. Yet her fingers bunched before she could stop them. Next thing she knew, she had risen onto her tiptoes and decked him in his handsome, though no longer clean-shaven, jaw. The bristle of his whiskers chafed her skin as his face and her fist collided.

He clutched the spot her hand had bounced off of, injuring her knuckles in the process. "What was that for?"

"If you're here, you're a big fat liar." Steam had built within her in a flash. Now vented, she sagged under the relieved pressure. "I don't understand. Why? I cried buckets when your dad told me you'd gone to enjoy your freedom. That you'd left without bothering to say goodbye. That you didn't plan to come home because there was nothing important for you there. That you were enjoying the high life, the parties, the women. And here you are, six hours from Windsor...driving a tow truck? This is crazy. The whole world is flipping nuts."

Whether it was because of dehydration, the shock or the devastation at discovering her supposed best friend's ultimate betrayal—or maybe all of those factors together—Kaelyn felt as though she were watching herself from a distance.

"Hey. I'm actually a mechanic. The truck is..." Bryce trailed off, probably spotting her glazed eyes. He lunged for her again, attempting to steady her as she listed to the left. "Are you okay? You look like you're going to pass—"

His concern became garbled as her eyelids grew heavy. Her knees buckled. At least the grass would make a soft landing pad, again, she thought.

Yet when she blinked against the bright sun swimming above, it didn't seem like much time had passed and she definitely wasn't sprawled on the ground. No, those were muscled arms cradling her against a very hard chest. One that had nothing in common with gentlemen she'd held at an appropriate distance while waltzing during her father's social functions. Or even the handful she'd invited to share her bed.

She attempted to protest, to keep herself separate from the guy she would have wanted—far too much—to come to her rescue if given a single wish. Though she'd figured it impossible. Maybe she'd hit her head when her tire had blown. Maybe this was some sick trick of her mind, recalling the one person who'd always had her back when she needed him most. Except transformed into the kind of man who wouldn't place leisurely pursuits above hard work, dedication and loyalty.

That had to be it. He was a figment of her imagination.

Kaelyn reached way up and pinched his thick neck. Hard.

"Ouch! What the hell?" He glared at her.

A combination whimper and chuckle left her parched throat. She didn't know whether to laugh or cry. Both seemed imminent. The chaos in her mind had her yearning to black out again. So she surrendered. Kaelyn allowed herself to be weak and lean on Bryce as she'd longed to do so many times in his decade-long absence. "Making sure you're real."

"Come on, your majesty. Let me hoist your chariot onto the flatbed and we'll get the hell out of here. I'm taking you home."

"No! You can't make me go back." Despite the futility, she attempted to thrash and squirm from his unrelenting grip. "Please."

"Hush. What has you so scared, Kae? I don't mean your father's house. I'm taking you to my place. Where you'll be safe. I swear. We can work out the rest later." Bryce didn't really give her a choice in the matter. He made it easy to surrender, though she hated letting him take care of her. Right when she'd vowed to gain control of her life, her choices, her future. "Whatever has you freaked out, I'll take care of it. I promise I'll fix it. I'll—"

"Stop talking." Here she was, in the arms of another bastard who'd lied to her.

For her own good.

She must have growled against his neck—which smelled amazing, damn him.

When he chuckled, rumbling against her ear, she balled her fists and thumped them against his chest. A waste of effort. The ineffective blows rained over him without denting his resilient muscles. "Okay. Whatever it takes. Settle down."

She tried, but her newly honed survival instincts screamed at her to run.

He held her tighter. "I get that you're pissed. I didn't mean to laugh. But you always were adorable when you got mad. Some things never change, I guess."

Before she could lash out again, he shocked her by dropping a light kiss on her forehead.

"I missed you, Kae," he murmured. "Every day."

ABOUT THE AUTHOR

Jayne Rylon is a *New York Times* and *USA Today* bestselling author. She received the 2011 RomanticTimes Reviewers' Choice Award for Best Indie Erotic Romance.

Her stories used to begin as daydreams in seemingly endless business meetings, but now she is a full-time author, who employs the skills she learned from her straight-laced corporate existence in the business of writing. She lives in Ohio with two cats and her husband, the infamous Mr. Rylon.

When she can escape her purple office, Jayne loves to travel the world, SCUBA dive, take pictures, avoid speeding tickets in her beloved Sky and—of course—read.